I0452368

Guardians of Earth II

Book Two: The Watcher

P. R. Garcia

Please leave an honest review on Amazon.

DEDICATION

This book is dedicated to Ronald Reau, a cherished colleague with whom I had the privilege of working with for many years. After reading Guardians of Earth—Book One: The Argus, Mr. Reau expressed his desire to journey into space in one of my future books. The character of Ron Reau in this book is the fulfillment of that wish. While the character takes on a unique life within these pages, it stands as a testament to the inspiration Ronald Reau provided me and is not intended to represent the real Mr. Reau

.

If you would like more information about her books or to join her Newsletter, please go to:

https://prgarcia1.com

We all die.

The goal isn't to live forever,

The goal is to

Create something that will.

Chuck Palahniuk

CONTENTS

Chapter 1: THE CRIME

"Have you lost your minds?" Jeremy burst into the room, eyes wide with disbelief. The tantalizing aroma of cooking meat hit him, making his mouth water. He slammed the security door shut with a bang that echoed through the room. "Eating meat is forbidden on the Space Station. You all know that."

"Don't get all security guard on us," Henry said, tossing Jeremy a chicken leg. "It's just food."

Jeremy couldn't remember the last time he smelled, let alone tasted, real meat. "Where did you ever get this?" His stomach growled in repulsiveness and his face scrunched into a look of disgust as a horrible thought entered his mind. "Please tell me this isn't dog. You didn't slaughter a few of the dogs running around this station, did you?"

Ron laughed loudly. "Don't worry; those four-legged critters are safe. At least for the moment." He laughed again as he bit into the chicken breast he was holding.

"What is it?"

"Chicken!"

"Shh, keep it down, Harry warned. "If we get caught, there will be hell to pay."

Jeremy stared at the chicken leg in his hand. He inhaled the intoxicating aroma. It smelt so good. A drop of saliva slipped from his mouth and down his cheek. He wiped the droll away with his hand, then onto his shirt. Should he indulge or do the right thing?

"They won't lock you up for one little leg," Ron said.

Against his better judgment, Jeremy cautiously bit into the chicken leg. He kept it on his tongue, savoring the flavor before swallowing it. "Oh, It tastes as good as it smells. But, Ron, where did you get chickens?"

"Remember Glogg's announcement that they were bringing some animals out of suspension? Some of them must have gotten loose because when Harry and I were walking below yesterday, we found these chickens just meandering around," Ron answered. We didn't see any aliens with them, so we figured they were up for grabs. There was a pig, too. We tried to catch him, but he was too loud, so we had to let him go."

"Why do you call them that?" an irritated Jeremy asked.

"Call who what?"

"Call the caretakers 'aliens'? Can't you refer to them as Bobonos or just caretakers? Why are you also so disrespectful of them?"

Ron threw his empty chicken bone into the fire. "I hate those purple and green, bug-eyed aliens," Ron spat. "I hate them all."

"Why? They saved your life. They saved all our lives."

"I didn't ask to be saved." Ron squinted his eyes and grated his teeth together. "I wish they had left me on Earth with the rest of humanity. We had no proof Earth was going to end. I had a good life back there." Ron stepped forward. His foot grazed one of the small rocks encircling the fire pit carved in the dirt. The rock ricocheted off another rock and flew up into the air. It dropped into the pit, causing ash and hot embers to erupt.

Jeremy jumped to his feet and pulled off his shirt. "Quick. Fan those embers in the air away from the ceiling. They'll set off the fire alarms."

"You're such a worrier," Ron chuckled "Do you think I'd have a fire without disabling the fire alarm?"

"What do you mean you disabled the fire alarm?"

"Just what I said." Ron walked to a panel door on his left and opened it. "See, all taken care of."

Jeremy stared in disbelief at the cut wires hanging inside the opening. He rushed over, being careful not to trip over the fire. "Ron, tell me you didn't do this. Tell me you didn't sabotage the alarm system." Beads of sweat dotted his forehead.

"Relax, I'm not crazy enough to mess with the whole alarm system," Ron chuckled, a confident grin spreading across his face. "We just made a small adjustment to this room's sensors so the cooking heat wouldn't set them off. Everything else is completely secure."

"You idiot," Jeremy screamed. "You may have prevented a fire alarm from sounding, but you triggered a malfunction notification. Security is already on their way to investigate."

"I'm getting out of here before those robot security guys arrive," Jake announced as he ran towards the door.

"Me too." Ron grabbed a handful of chicken and followed.

"No, wait." Jeremy grabbed Ron's arm. "We must put this fire out. We can't just leave it. Without the fire detectors to put it out, it might spread through the entire vessel."

"Then you put it out," Ron said. "I can't afford to get into any more trouble with Glock."

"Fine." Using a chicken leg bone, Jeremy separated the embers away from each other. They were glowing red hot. He threw handfuls of sand onto the scorched wood, hoping to smother it.

Ron stopped at the door and looked back. Jeremy was right. Even if he hated living on the damn station, he couldn't jeopardize his mom and sister's lives. "You'll need some water too." He rushed past his friend, retrieved the water container they had brought, and sat it beside Jeremy. Kneeling also, he pushed sand and dirt over the embers. "We can't pour the water on until we get some embers out. Otherwise, it will just make a lot of steam and smoke."

A soft swishing sound filled the room as a mist of fine anti-flame retardant drifted down from the ceiling, squelching the fire.

"Cover your mouth and nose," a voice said through the smoke. "And close your eyes. It's not good for humans to breathe the chemicals in. The room will clear shortly."

Jeremy and Ron covered their mouths and noses with their shirts. They closed their eyes and waited for the toxic mist to clear. Suddenly, someone grabbed both boys' arms and escorted them out of the room.

"Good day, Jeremy. I see you have managed to get into trouble with Ronald again."

"Hi, Xavier," Jeremy said. "Can we open our eyes now?"

"Yes."

Jeremy opened his eyes and gazed at the android beside him, his arm still in the android's grasp. He remained silent, unsure of what to say. Six security robots surrounded them, weapons drawn and pointed at them. A seventh robot exited the chemical-filled room and handed Xavier a half-eaten piece of meat and a handful of bones. Xavier lifted it to his nostrils and breathed in the unfamiliar smell. Using his specialized analyzing capabilities, he scrutinized the evidence. "Gallus domesticus; a Rhode Island Red, to be exact. One of the missing chickens." He placed the bone and pieces of uneaten chicken meat in an evidence bag. "Should I assume that all three chickens were eaten?"

"You'd have to ask Ronald," Jeremy sheepishly replied. Ronald said nothing.

"And what happened to the fire alarm?" Again, there was only silence. "Under Section 2B, subsection 3, building a fire aboard the station is a capital offense. As is subsection 18c, no one may tamper with an alarm. The theft of property violates Rule 128, Section 5, paragraph 15. Unfortunately, there is no rule outlawing the consumption of animal flesh. What do you have to say?"

"I'm sorry," Jeremy said, his voice catching in his throat. Why did he always let Ronald drag him into these situations?

"What about you, Mr. Reau?" Xavier said "Are you sorry, too? Do you have anything to say today?"

Ronald ground his teeth together as he kicked the floor. He had plenty to say but now was not the time.

"Your parents are being notified as we speak. Zeibberk and Rignea, handcuff the prisoners. Put them with the others."

———————

Glogg sat at his desk, staring at the door, waiting for Xavier to arrive with the culprits. Learning that Ronald and his gang had caused the malfunction didn't surprise him, but the fact that Jeremy was with them shocked him. In all his years as commander, he had never needed to hold court over those on the station. Sure, there had been minor infractions, but nothing to demand a stiff sentence. But ever since this new group of humans came aboard, his office had repeatedly served as a place for disciplinary actions. And it usually involved Ronald.

The human inhabitants were born at the station and had decades to adjust to living in a space station or having the chance to return to Earth. But the new humans brought aboard when they left Earth only had hours to decide. Some, like Ronald and his family, only had minutes to decide if they wanted a life in space or to remain on Earth. Most new arrivals adapted well to living in a sphere and were valuable assets to the collective. Others had difficulty making the transition.

Ronald was the younger brother of Jeremy's ex-girlfriend, Racheal. The boy had trouble acclimating to the confinement, rules, and a totally vegan diet. He was rebellious, anti-authority, argumentative, and disrespectful to anyone who was not human. Within the first month of their voyage, he gathered other newcomers unhappy with their surroundings, and they had been causing problems for the past four and a half years.

Did Ronald hold him and the other aliens responsible for the catastrophic end of Earth? It was a thought that had been gnawing at Glogg for months, and he couldn't shake off the guilt that consumed him. It wasn't like they lost the battle with the Kett on purpose. Hell, he lost his only three sons in the siege. He had to take the Space Station away and leave Earth undefended. Their cargo of Earth's animals and plants was their priority. Why couldn't these disenchanted humans realize that? Plus, it was up to Earth's inhabitants to decide if they wanted another orbiting station from the Interstellar Space Coalition. Not his. All they had to do was change and stop the fighting and destruction of their planet.

But it didn't matter why Ron and his followers broke the rules today. Their actions put the entire station at risk and destroyed valuable animals. Glogg believed that Ronald and his friends stole the three chickens, hoping to eat something other than the regular vegetarian diet. They thought they had found a secure spot to cook their meal, but the station had surveillance installed everywhere to detect irregularities. Whoever cut the alarm wires only alerted security to the problem, and the smell of cooking meat had already alerted security that something was amiss. Nothing went unnoticed on the station.

As he waited, Glogg thoughtfully deliberated on the various choices before him. Despite his belief in Jeremy's innocence, they found him with the others. And the fact that he was his top commander, Renn's grandson, could not sway his decisions. The five young men had all committed crimes carrying the death penalty. Even though his race did not believe in capital punishment, the original ISC travelers had incorporated the sentence into their laws to safeguard the station. Glogg was sure they never meant for such a penalty to be carried out. Could he sentence Ron, Jeremy, and the others to execution? Could he kill his best friend's grandson?

Glogg knew one thing for sure - Ronald's latest indiscretion made him too big a liability to allow him to live freely on the station. They could not release him once they arrived at New Earth. As for the others, Glogg would judge Jeremy and the other three on their merits.

A firm knock at the door broke his thought. "Enter."

The door opened, and a handcuffed Ronald was pushed through. Xavier followed, pushing him to the chair before Glogg's desk and forcing him down. Three more guards emerged with three bound humans and placed them against the wall to await their sentencing.

"Only three?" Glogg asked. "I thought there were four?"

"There were," Xavier answered, laying the evidence on Glogg's desk. "Henry bolted when we got there. He's hiding somewhere in the station. Juaquin and a few others are looking for him as we speak."

"It's a damn space station," Glogg shouted. "Where in the hell does he think he can hide?"

"Who knows?" Xavier replied. "He's been taking flying lessons with Jeremy, so I have assigned extra security to the aircraft bunker."

"The bunker? Do you think he's crazy enough to try to leave the station?"

"Not crazy enough, Sir, but possibly scared enough."

Glogg locked eyes with Ronald, a look of hate and anger visible. "Mr. Reau, as doubtful as it is, it is possible that you did not kill the chickens, start a fire, or cut the alarm wiring. I do not want to presume your guilt. Do you do these things?"

Once more, Ronald remained silent.

"I will ask you one more time. Are you guilty or innocent?"

Ronald looked down at the floor.

"Do you know what danger you put this station in by building that fire?"

"It was only a little fire," Ronald murmured.

"IT WAS A FIRE!" Glogg screamed, making the young man jump. "There is oxygen being piped into all parts of this space station. Oxygen burns. Did you know that?" There was no answer. "DID YOU KNOW THAT?"

"Yes."

"Yet you built a fire to cook a chicken right under one of the engines and a huge tube of flammable fuel," Glogg continued. "Did you know that?"

Ron turned and looked at Harry. "You said there wasn't anything dangerous above us?"

"I didn't think there was." Harry shrugged his shoulders.

"Didn't know or didn't want to know?" Glogg asked, now looking over at Harry.

Suddenly, the door flew open, and a breathless Renn and Steven burst into the room. "Sorry we're late," Renn announced, breathing in gulps of air. "What are the charges?" He turned his attention to Jeremy, but the young man would not return his grandfather's or father's glances.

"Violation of Section 2B, subsection 3, building. Subsection 18c disconnecting an alarm. Rule 128, Section 5, paragraph 15, taking of station property," Xavier stated. "And most damning, Section 2B, subsection 3, building a fire. I apprehended him myself."

"A fire? You built a fire?" Renn stared, his heart beating faster. He knew that crime of making a fire carried the death penalty. He couldn't believe, Jeremy's guilt but Xavier apprehended him alongside Ronald and the rest. He had to do something. "Might we talk in private, Glogg?"

Glogg thought for a moment. There was little doubt that these young men were guilty, but perhaps Renn had a solution that didn't involve death—at least, Glogg hoped so. Besides, he owed his friend a chance to save Jeremy.

"Xavier, have your men take these four to the holding room," Glogg ordered "You remain and give me an account of what you found. Renn, you too may stay, but Steven is to go."

"No, but I . . ." Steven stuttered.

"You go with Jeremy." Renn quickly said cutting Steven off. He did not want to give Glogg the chance to change his mind. "This is something I have to handle."

Chapter 2: IT'S NO ONE'S FAULT

Xavier detailed his findings meticulously, sticking strictly to the facts without making assumptions or offering opinions.

"Just young men letting off steam, stretching their wings," Renn suggested.

"Not this time," Glogg interjected. "This time, they endangered everyone on this ship."

"Surely, you pulled a few stunts in your youth," Renn countered

"Never. I had more pride in my family, our way of life, and the rules."

Renn knew Glogg told the truth. His friend never bent a rule, let alone broke one. He hoped his commander would bend the rules this time, for Jeremy's life depended upon it.

"I understand Ron endangered the station. But he didn't do it on purpose. He believed the room to be safe. The kid hungered for meat and saw an opportunity to quench his craving."

"His appetite is not a very good defense."

"I agree," Renn said. "But we have to consider the circumstances. We uprooted him from his home planet, brought him to an entirely alien environment, and abandoned his planet to its fate. He had no choice in the matter and no time to adjust. That has to account for something."

"It does, and it is the only reason he and the others are still alive. The moment the security androids apprehended them, they should have executed them. Thankfully, Xavier factored Ron's past experiences into his judgment. Coupled with the bond he shares with you, it led him to consider the appropriate punishment carefully. Glogg, lost in thought, walked to the window and stared out into the endless expanse of space. Some days he wished he had chosen a different line of employment.

"I understand your dilemma. Ron has broken the rules a few times, making it hard to know what to do," Renn replied.

"A few times?" Glogg asked. "Fifty times is not a few."

"This is number eighty-two," Xavier said. "And we didn't even count the ones from the first six months."

"We don't need your corrections," Renn sneered.

"And each infraction is worse than the previous," Glogg continued, ignoring Xavier's comment. "I can't excuse his antics to inexperience or the fact he didn't have time to assimilate anymore. It's been almost five years. More than enough time has passed for him to adjust."

"Not if he doesn't want to be here," Renn said. "Every day, he resents being brought here. Every day, he is reminded of what and who he left behind. Every day, he realizes the Earth he loves may be no more. Could you accept all that?"

"Yes, just like I accepted the death of my three sons," Glogg said, a tear sliding down his cheek "He's not a boy anymore, Renn. He's a grown man. And he needs to be responsible. After this, how can I ever trust him? How can I trust him once we land on New Earth? The animals will roam the landscape. How can I let Mr. Reau roam free to slaughter them?"

"We can't," Renn replied, facing the truth. "Mr. Reau will require heavy monitoring and supervision. If a few chickens enticed him, what would he do with an entire planet of eatable animals?"

"Precisely," Glogg sighed, the burden of the law heavy on his shoulders. "To safeguard the future, Mr. Reau's punishment is clear. Fire and alarm infractions are capital offenses, as you well know. Each carries the mandatory sentence of death, which should be carried out immediately."

"But that's where I differ," Renn countered swiftly, his words tumbling out in a rush. "The death penalty, while established law, feels like a misinterpretation of our forefathers' intent. Killing him will only spark a revolt among his followers."

"And not imposing the sentence will have others believing the rules don't have to be followed," Xavier added. "Other humans may try to slaughter and eat the few animals we have awakened."

"So, this is a human problem?" Renn asked, giving Xavier a disapproving scowl.

"Yes. Only humans wish to eat animal flesh. None of the other species have such food in their diet."

"It's not a human problem," Glogg shouted. "It's a station problem. We can't allow anyone, regardless of their species, to break the rules." Glogg returned to his seat behind the desk. "I recommend we judge each of the five, including Jeremy, on their merits and shortcomings. Can we determine who stole the chickens, who disarmed the fire alarms, and who built the fire?"

"Unlikely," Xavier replied. "That room contained no surveillance equipment. I can test the wiring for DNA. We might determine which human was responsible."

"It's doubtful that would give us enough proof. More than likely, it was either Harry or Ralph who cut the wires," Renn stated.

"Why do you say that?" Glogg asked.

"Ronald doesn't have the expertise for such an operation. But I suspect he is the one who captured the chickens and built the fire."

"I concur," Xavier said. "Ronald is the brawn of the operations, not the brains. As for Jeremy, I believe he is guilty through association only. Your grandson and I were together all day working on the designs for the new UPB-46. He didn't leave the area until fifteen hundred, right after his communicator beeped. He informed me he needed to take care of some business and would return in two hours."

"So, Jeremy is innocent of the charges?" Renn asked. "And since eating animal flesh is not a crime, he should be freed. Don't you both agree?"

"Except he is guilty by association," Glogg said. "He might have had prior knowledge of the crimes and choose not to report it."

"Is that what you believe? That Jeremy was an accomplice?"

"No, not really," Glogg confessed. "But I have no way to determine what he did and therefore cannot determine his role in this."

"Ask them," Renn shouted.

"What?"

"Ask them," Renn repeated. "Interview each of the five and ask them what they did and did not do."

"They'll never tell on the others."

"They don't have to. Just have them tell you what they themselves did."

Glogg turned to Xavier. "You're the head of security. What do you think?"

"While I think some will lie to save themselves, I believe Jeremy, Ronald, and possibly Henry will be honest about what they did. That is if we ever find Henry. I've noted a kinship between Jeremy and the other two. If the others are innocent and they are not, I believe each will be truthful to protect the others."

"Make it so," Glogg ordered. "Xavier, I need you to personally interview these four individuals to uncover the truth and find Henry."

"Yes, Sir."

"We will meet back here in three hours and discuss our options. Renn, I need you to stay."

Once Xavier left, Glogg's demeanor changed. "Renn, I will do anything I can to spare Jeremy's life. I love him as one of my own and see a future for him as a pilot and aircraft designer. Xavier gives him high marks."

"I know you do. And I apologize for the situation my grandson and the others have put you in."

"Why? You had nothing to do with their antics."

"No, but I feel responsible. One culprit is my grandson; the others are here because I insisted we not leave Rachel and her brother behind. We wouldn't be in this predicament had I not intervened."

"It was the right thing to do." Glogg gave his friend a warm smile. "Even though Jeremy and Rachel's relationship did not work out, you allowed your grandson to discover whether she was his true love or not. That's all any of us can ask for. Plus, I understand she is a marvelous medical student and has developed several ways already to help the Caladrine with their plant allergies. If we can harness Mr. Reau's abilities for a positive purpose, he has the potential to become a significant contributor to the colony."

"But how do we do that?"

"That's exactly what I want you to find out." Glogg gave him a mischievous smile, the kind that made Renn uneasy, knowing he wouldn't like what was coming next. "I want you to work with Sarina and Steven to figure out how to handle this guy. They're experienced with humans and might know how to get through to him. I've had no luck, but maybe they can."

"That's a pretty tall order," Renn replied. "I fear Ronald suffers from what many Earth humans suffer from."

"What is that?"

"Indifference and the belief you can take whatever you want."

"I don't think that's it. When I told him that the X-17 engine and fuel vat were located above their position, I saw a flicker of concern and remorse in his eyes. I don't believe he would have started the fire if he had known. Besides, I suspect there's another reason driving his anger."

"What reason?"

"Not dying," Glogg suggested. "Everyone he left behind faced an uncertain future. Either an alien race will harvest Earth, or the humans will destroy it themselves. Ron feels guilty because he has escaped their fate."

"Is it possible he's seeking death deliberately?"

"That's what I want you, Sarina, and Steven to tell me."

"Have you heard any news from the ISC? Will they send another space station to guard Earth?"

"I received a communication this morning," Glogg said. "It stated that the satellites we left to monitor the humans showed that fighting restarted in the Middle East. Communication between the NATO countries and Russia suggests war is a strong possibility. Thirty percent of the rainforests are now leveled. And the oceans have risen three inches since our departure because of glaciers melting."

"They never learn, do they?" Renn prepared to open the door, then paused. "What happens if we can't reach him?

"If he cannot be swayed, I have no alternative than to grant him his wish and sentence him to death."

———————

Renn strolled down the hallways towards the holding room. Due to Ronald and his friends' infractions, three small offices were fitted with bars and converted into jail cells. Once or twice a month, Ron spent time in the cells. But his previous offenses were minor infractions, and he was set free after two or three days. This time, he faced the real possibility of death. Could he, Stephen, or Sarina reach this young man in time?

Renn entered the holding area. Ron and Tobias occupied the first cell, Harry and Ralph the second, and no one was in the third.

"Where is Jeremy? And Stephen?" Renn asked.

"I am confident Jeremy is not guilty of the serious charges and was just in the wrong place at the wrong time," Xavier said. I sent him home under his father's care and supervision."

"Thanks, Xavier. I appreciate it."

"Don't thank me yet, Renn, because one or more of these young men might face death for these crimes. And Glogg will decide Jeremy's punishment."

Renn squeezed Xavier's arm as he walked past. "Thanks for not carrying out the mandatory sentencing when you found him and the others."

"Is Glogg going to kill Ronald?" Jeremy shouted the moment Renn entered the room. "You can't let Glogg kill him."

"I don't know," Renn confessed. "But you have to understand the seriousness of your friend's crimes. The laws he and the others broke each carry the death penalty."

"But Ron wasn't aware of the severity of their actions," Jeremy shouted.

"He should have. They all should have. I witnessed Xavier explain security protocols and their penalties to the new arrivals the day they arrived."

"He received that talk five years ago. How can you expect Ron to remember everything Xavier told him and the others?"

"You do." Jeremy remained silent, a heavy weight settling on his shoulders. His grandfather's words echoed in the sterile room: "Just like on Earth, Jeremy, ignorance of the law isn't an excuse. He took a reckless gamble, jeopardizing this entire station. Starting a fire could have been catastrophic. His actions demand immediate and decisive consequences."

"Can you do anything to help?" Sarina asked, her face soaked with tears, her eyes swollen, and her skin tinted red. "Steven said Jeremy could receive the same sentencing as the others?"

"That is a possibility." Renn glanced around the room. "Where are Timmy and Mary?"

"When we learned of Jeremy's arrest, Jenny took them to the Recreation Room to play with their friends," Sarina explained.

"That's my Jenny." Renn smiled, but it did not last long. His features were overshadowed by a direct, unyielding gaze that left no room for misunderstanding. "Let's sit down. Jeremy, I need you to tell me everything that you witnessed and what you participated in. I can't help if I am unaware of the truth."

"You don't believe he helped with starting that fire?" Sarina asked.

"No, but I need to hear him say it," Renn said. "Jeremy, were you aware that Ron or one of the others took the chickens? Or did you take part in their capture?"

"No, I didn't. And Ron didn't steal the chickens. He found them wandering down a hallway below."

"I believe you," Renn said. "But this news adds another dimension to our problems. If the chickens wandered off alone, the security fence holding them must have malfunctioned. It is possible additional animals are free and roaming the ship." Renn paused, collecting his thoughts before asking, "What about the slaughter of the chickens and the making of the fire? Did you participate in either?"

"Possibly," Jeremy mumbled, his voice barely a whisper.

Sarina's breath caught. Her eyes widened, searching her son's face for a flicker of truth, a hint of the guilt that gnawed at her gut. "Jeremy?" she breathed, her voice trembling.

Steven's gaze sharpened. "Possibly what?" he asked, his booming voice suddenly small in the sterile room.

Jeremy locked eyes with his father, the man whose unwavering pride had always been his guiding light. Now, shame burned in his chest, a suffocating weight threatening to pull him under. Could that pride survive the truth he held? He swallowed hard, the words stuck in his throat, a bitter confession waiting to be released.

"Ron asked to meet yesterday, but I was too tired after working with Xavier all day. We've been putting in some major hours and are just days away from constructing the new aircraft. Xavier said I can help build it." He noticed the anxiety on the adults' faces as they waited for his answer. "Anyway, Ron called again last night and woke me. He said he needed a quiet place where he could get some sleep, a place without sensors. He has insomnia again. I was half asleep and, without thinking, blurted out the location of the room I used to hide in when I needed to escape, especially after Rachel and I broke up."

"That's why we could never locate you," Renn said. "It used to drive me crazy how you just disappeared off the grid."

"I heard you and Dad talk about how almost every part of this place was bugged. It took me six months to locate an area without surveillance cameras."

"I don't understand," Renn said. "How did you figure it out? No maps show these areas, and even I know only a few of them."

"Some know them all," Jeremy confessed, his voice low.

"The RZ-47G's," Renn said, his eyes narrowing as he turned to face his grandson. "You figured out a way to trick Xavier into revealing where one was located, didn't you? You used his fondness for you against his security protocols."

"Yes."

"Why would you do that?" Sarina asked.

"It felt like you were suffocating me," Jeremy blurted out. "You were always trying to get me to do something. Back on Earth, I had my life, my friends, everything I'd built. Leaving it all behind felt like losing a part of myself. I just wanted some space, some time to breathe, but you wouldn't let up."

"I'm sorry, Jeremy," Stephen said. "But that still didn't give you the right to trick Xavier."

"I know. And I think Xavier figured it out. I only visited the secret place four times before Xavier found me. He said he needed my help in designing a new flier. Somehow, I think he realized the emotional turmoil I was experiencing. We began working on the flier that day, and I never returned to that room. I actually forgot about it until Ron called."

"Did you have anything to do with the slaughtering of the chickens or the building of the fire?" Renn asked.

"I didn't know about either until I opened the door. Ron texted me around fourteen hundred, saying he needed to see me immediately and to come to the secret room. I realized my mistake in telling him about the place and planned on telling you, Grandfather, about it. But when I got there, the smell of cooking meat was more than I could resist. I hadn't smelled such a delightful smell since we left Earth almost five years ago. I didn't know it was chicken until Ron told me. I figured they were already dead and saw no harm in having a taste?"

"The harm was they were cooking them over an open fire. An unsecured FIRE, Jeremy." Renn paused again as he took several paces. "I need you to tell me. Who started it, and who put it out?"

"I don't know who started it. It was already in full flame when I arrived. But I put the fire out. Ron helped. If he hadn't, he would have gotten away."

"Why did you put it out?" Steven asked.

"Because the others ran, I knew how much damage an unattended fire could do. Believe me; I never forget we are floating in a vessel of explosible fuels."

"Why did Ronald stay?" Renn asked.

"Because he's my best friend. He would never desert me in a time of need."

"Let's hope you're right," Renn said. "Xavier is questioning him and the others as we speak. If they confirm your story, Glogg may only give you a light sentence, such as removing you from the UPB-46 project or denying your application to military training."

"No, he can't," Jeremy protested.

"Jeremy, even though you are innocent of Ron's crimes, you were aware of them," Renn stated. "You should have reported their actions when you discovered the fire. It's what a soldier would do. And don't use the excuse that Ron was your friend. A member of this complex has one priority — the welfare of the station and her occupants, including the animals and plants. You swore to protect this vessel when you joined the team last year. Did you not?"

"Yes," Jeremy said, holding his head up high. "You are right, Grandfather. I should have put the welfare of the station first, not my friendship. That is the vow I took. I will accept any punishment Glogg deems appropriate for me. I only ask you to save Ronald if you can."

Renn smiled at his grandson. "You are growing into a fine young man, Jeremy. The admission of your participation will influence Glogg's decision on the severity of your punishment. Caelifera honor loyalty over duty."

"So, if Ron is truthful when Xavier questions him, Glogg might be lenient?" Sarina asked.

"I'm afraid it's not that simple for our Mr. Reau," Renn said. "Ronald's indiscretions over the years are many, and each more serious than the last. Today, his actions could have destroyed the entire station and ended all our lives. But Glogg is not heartless. If he believes Ron can change, he will lessen his sentence even if it costs him his command."

"Why would sparing Ron's life cost him his command?" Stephen asked.

"Because the ISC may order his removal," Renn answered. "They may perceive his refusal to execute the required punishment as a break in Glogg's loyalty to the ISC."

"They would do that?"

"Yes. They may also demand he forfeit his life in exchange for the breach."

"His death will be on my head." Jeremy hung his head. "All this is because I thought I loved a girl and wouldn't leave her behind. Ronald wouldn't even be here if I hadn't shamed you into bringing Rachel up here."

Renn smiled. "I said those same words to Glogg. Except I said that the fault for bringing Rachel and the others here was mine. Do you know what Glogg told me? He said my assumption was incorrect. The fault wasn't mine or anyone else's. Love needed a chance to blossom. No matter what happens, remember that, Jeremy. You are not at fault. Each of us is responsible for our actions and decisions. Ronald is accountable for his. Glogg will be likewise accountable for his choice of action."

Chapter 3: MALFUNCTION

Three hours later, Renn and Xavier reported to Glogg's office. Too nervous to sit, Renn paced.

"The three males in holding confirmed what Jeremy told Renn," Xavier reported. "Jeremy was not involved with catching the chickens or building a fire. Mr. Reau had invited him down to the room under the pretense of wanting to share something important to him. Jeremy is absolved of all charges." Renn breathed a sigh of relief. "However, due to his oversight in reporting the incident, I concur that some punishment is mandated."

"Do you have a preference?" Glogg asked the android.

"Jeremy is a great asset to the UPB46 development team," Xavier replied. "Tomorrow at 0-eight hundred tomorrow, we start building the prototype. And his presence IS needed."

"Plus, delaying his induction into the military academy would ensure he can collaborate with you for another year," Renn added, smiling at his android friend.

"While true, I did not factor that into my assessment."

Renn laughed. "Xavier, you're becoming more human every day."

"I see no reason to insult me. I am simply stating the facts."

"I'm sure you are." Glogg turned to hide his smirk. "I deny Jeremy's application to the military academy for two years. If he redeems himself at the end of the first year, we will dismiss the second year. Renn, advise your grandson of my decision."

"Yes, Sir."

"I also learned the young men did not steal the chickens from the barnyard," Xavier continued. "Both Mr. Reau and Mr. Hallsworth stated they found the chickens walking down hall 32F, Subsection C."

"That's worrisome," Glogg commented. "How did they get out of the secured animal enclosure?"

"I asked them, and neither had an answer. They also reported a pig with the chickens but could not catch it.

"A pig?"

"Yes, Sir. To verify their story, I backtracked what I believed to be the chickens' route from the barnyard and discovered a most alarming scene. Two goats, four ducks, a ram, and four rabbits were outside their designated area. Upon inspection, I discovered a part of the fencing was missing."

"Missing?" a surprised Renn asked. "Like cut-away missing?"

"No. The fencing showed no signs of being tampered with or cut. It was simply gone. I believe there was a malfunction in its program, and part of the shield stopped working."

"Do you have any ideas about the cause?" Glogg asked. "We've never had a problem with any security field program."

"There was no apparent cause. I have alerted Master Kim of my findings. He and his team are investigating the problem as we speak."

"Have you located Mr. Reeves yet?"

"No, Sir. The young Henry still evades our capture. We glimpsed him on security camera 248, but he disappeared before we could find him. It's only a matter of time before we apprehend him. He can't elude our security measures forever."

"I want …" Before Glogg completed his sentence, the room shook as they heard a loud boom. Alarms sounded. "What in the hell was that?"

"Number 346 reports an explosion in engine room 15," Xavier reported. "He reports that the fire inhibitors are not working. They are trying to put it out manually. I am also getting reports stating that the outside wall has ruptured, and an immense hole now occupies the space where engine eighteen once sat. The explosion blew three crew personnel into space. Four more died of asphyxiation." Xavier paused for a moment. "I just issued a station-wide lockdown. All life forms must immediately move to the front biosphere. If the station becomes unstable, I will eject the biosphere and notify ISC that you require immediate evacuation."

Glogg wanted to argue that he needed to see what was happening below for himself, but he knew Xavier was right. If systems were malfunctioning, any part of the space station could lose pressurization or air quality without warning. The only safe place for everyone was inside the sealed room.

"Very well. I must stop by my apartment and get Una."

"She and Renn's family are already being escorted to the room. You two must proceed to the front biosphere immediately."

Glogg opened his side desk drawer and removed the control pad. "Glogg confirmation 83-C-45-Z Transfer controls to pad 852."

"Transfer complete."

"What of the animals?" Renn asked. "If the station is lost, we will lose all the specimens."

"They built the Habitat Sphere as a separate biosphere for this type of situation," Xavier said. "It contains a separate life-support system and generators. Its wiring does not connect to the primary station, so it should not be affected. If necessary, I will eject it as well. Now go."

———————————

"Dad, what's happening?" Sarina ran up to her father the moment he entered the room.

"There's been a malfunction in one of the engine rooms," Renn explained. "A sensor failed, causing one of the fuel tanks to explode and fracture the outer wall. We're safe in here."

"But what if the station fails?" Tim asked.

"Believe it or not, this room is a spaceship inside the space station. It manufactures its own air and runs on an independent power source. If something happens, we will float out of the station and continue independently."

"I have to get Mary," Sarina shouted. "She's working today with Dr. Fiddlewit in the Habitat Sphere."

"Don't worry. She's okay." Renn said with a reassuring smile. "Don't worry. She's okay," Renn said with a reassuring smile. "The Habitat Sphere is a separate biosphere. If circumstances dictate it, the Habitat Sphere will also eject and rendezvous with the smaller station in an emergency."

"But I need to get her," Sarina insisted.

"Sweetheart, you can't leave," Renn replied.

"I'll go," Jenny stated. "I don't need air to breathe. I'll ensure she's all right and remain with her until this crisis ends. I will notify Renn when I reach her."

"Be careful," Renn said as he kissed his Jenny. "You may be all circuits and algorithms, but you're still the love of my life."

"As you are mine," Jenny replied. Without another word, she turned and left. The Spallings watched as she disappeared through the entrance door. Before the door closed, two police robots escorting Ronald, Harry, and Tobias entered the room, their wrists and ankles shackled.

"Are leg irons necessary?" Jeremy asked as he neared his friends.

"Protocol dictates that we secure all prisoners. Mr. Reau has a habit of disappearing."

"Don't worry about it," Ron said as he sat on a bench. Do you know what's going on? These two wouldn't tell us anything except that we must remain sequestered."

"A malfunction of some kind. An explosion blew out a section of the outer wall."

"Did we cause that?" Tobias's legs trembled. Unable to remain standing, he plopped down beside Ronald.

"I don't think so," Jeremy answered, but not in a convincing voice. "It occurred on the other side of the station. But I suppose one or two of those embers we kicked up could have traveled through the ventilation shafts."

"Don't even suggest such a thing," Ron whispered. "I'm in enough trouble without being responsible for destroying the entire station."

"Thanks for telling Xavier I had nothing to do with the chickens or the fire," Jeremy said.

"You didn't," Ron replied. "There was no reason to pull you down, too. At least one of us should have a future."

"Don't say that."

"It's true. Did your grandfather tell you what sentence Glogg is going to impose? Am I going to die?"

Overhearing the conversation, Renn drew closer to the prisoners. "Glogg, Xavier, and I were preparing to discuss your punishment when the explosion happened. If I didn't know better, I'd say you had something to do with it to keep Glogg from deciding." He winked and smiled.

"That's not even funny, Mr. Tensley."

"Captain Tensley."

"Sorry, Sir. Captain Tensley."

Jeremy watched as his grandfather's body grew rigid, the muscles on his face growing taut and strained. His eyes widen, filling with tears. "Jenny." Renn ran to the door and tried to exit.

"Commander, no living organism may leave," the sentry stated without emotion.

"My Jenny's in danger. I have to go." A firm grip clasped his shoulder. He turned to see Glogg standing beside him.

"Renn, you can't leave."

"Jenny's in trouble. I must go to her." Glogg's grip tightened." I can't lose Jenny again."

Glogg lifted his tablet and entered his command code. "Xavier, I need you to find Jenny. She went to check on Mary in the animal habitat. I believe she's in trouble. Send security to locate her and send someone to stay with Mary."

"Aye, Sir," came the voice over the control.

"Come, my friend," Glogg said. "Xavier will do what I cannot allow you to do - save your Jenny." Renn looked up at his friend, who towered over him. Despite Renn's height of six foot two, he was no match for Glogg's towering height of ten foot two. "Moreover, I cannot let you leave me to deal with all these Earth humans alone. You may not die for another six months until we arrive at New Earth."

"Who said anything about dying?" Renn said, a slight smile on his lips. "I plan on you retiring when we arrive and me becoming Head Commander."

Glogg chuckled. "Let's sit by the window and discuss your world of disillusionment."

———————

The expansive opening in the space station's outside wall forced Jenny to take a longer route to reach the Containment Sphere. She cut through the third-floor greenhouse and took the airlift at the east entrance to the fifth floor. She exited and ran down a long corridor to the E-6 security airlift. Upon entering, she pushed the second-floor button. She was thankful that, as an android, she did not get anxious because this journey took three times as long as it should. The elevator groaned and shook as it descended. She could hear the gears and chains grinding.

"Hold together," she said aloud. "I'm almost there."

Within seconds, the airlift's floor buckled, throwing her into the air. Jenny slammed into the ceiling and crashed onto the cold floor. Quickly running a diagnostic of her body, she determined she had sustained no injuries and stood. Listening, she could tell the airlift was not moving. Rising, she pushed the black button with a white number 2, but the airlift remained motionless. She tried pushing the remaining numbered buttons but to no avail. Walking to the doors, she placed her fingertips in the grove where the two airlift doors met and pulled the doors apart. As they opened, an echo of metallic vibrations and grinding friction filled the lift to reveal a wall of cold metal. She had stopped between floors.

"Xavier, can you hear me? I am in the security airlift E-6. It has malfunctioned. I am between floors, which ones I do not know. I estimate I am either between the fifth and fourth floors or the fourth and third floors. Can you assist?"

Jenny heard only silence.

"Xavier, can you hear me? Are you receiving my transmission?"

No reply.

"This is Android 685. I need assistance. All available androids, please reply."

Again, there was only silence.

"Damn. Communications must still be down."

She leaped up and hit the ceiling's exit door open. Jumping again, she grasped the edge of the door and pulled herself up onto the canopy of the airlift. Fortunately, the airlift was only eight inches above the fourth floor. Unfortunately, the doors were six inches too far from her reach. She surveyed the walls. They were as smooth as glass, nothing to grasp or hold onto. Looking over the edge at the chasm below the airlift, she knew jumping was not an option. She needed a bridge.

Jenny re-entered the airlift and tore off a long, wide piece of metal from the wall. The lift shook violently again. Knowing she only had seconds, she pushed the piece of metal through the escape hatch's opening and leaped up. She lifted the plank and jammed it into the space below the airlift doors. As she stepped onto the piece, the lift slipped. Using all her android strength, she ran up the plank, grabbed the doors, forced them open, and threw herself onto the corridor floor. Before hitting the floor with a loud thump, she heard the airlift fall, crashing into a subfloor below.

The corridor had suffered substantial damage. Large chunks of ceiling tiles littered the floor. Wiring and cables hung down from the ceiling like vines in a jungle. Doors were hanging askew. Jenny would have to reach the biosphere from another route.

Walking as fast as possible, Jenny dodged around tile pieces and ducked beneath wires and cables. After only ten yards, she froze. The almost inaudible sound of air escaping had triggered an internal alarm. She switched to thermal X-ray vision and examined the area but could not see any fractures. Cautiously, she took another step. And a second. The sound grew louder. And it was getting stronger. Titling her head ever so slightly, she triangulated the location of the sound. It was behind a service door three yards ahead.

Cautiously, Jenny approached the location. She felt around the panel's edge and detected no air being omitted. She listened again. It was the source of the sound. She opened the panel and found no cracks. The crack must be behind the panel. Pushing her fingers into the wall, she gently pulled the panel from its foundation to reveal a crack expanding with each passing second. Inside the crack, specks of light twinkled in a sea of black – stars. Another rupture. A result of the first breach or a new one? Not knowing if communications were still down, she hastily sent another message to notify Xavier of her dilemma. She also sent a message to Renn in case this was the end for her. She knew that within minutes, or even seconds, the crack would widen enough to suck this part of the station and her out into space. She would drift far away, never to see her Renn or her family again, condemned to an eternity of blackness.

The hissing intensified. An intense pressure began pulling her forward towards the hole. Jenny shifted her weight, but she could not stop her advancement. She jumped and reached for a pair of hanging cables as the wall burst open. But the rush of escaping air pulled the cables beyond her reach. Jenny slammed into the wall and clawed at the smooth walls as the void of space beckoned. With nothing to grab, the suction of escaping air pulled her outside the space station, propelling her further away from the station with each second. A sheath of frost enveloped her form as the chill of space embraced her. Although her body was artificial and devoid of blood, a warm fluid flowed within her veins. This fluid was now cooling, solidifying. Could this be the end for her? Her sight was failing. The station had become nothing more than a blur. Would Renn ever discover what happened to her?

"Hold on, Jenny. I've got you." Jenny could not see who her rescuer was, but she recognized Xavier's voice. She tried to speak, but her mouth was frozen, her vocal cords unyielding. "I'll have you back inside in just a few minutes." Jenny heard Xavier's jetpack as he held the female android in his arms and raced towards the opening. Jenny snuggled closer, the heat of his body warming the coldness in hers. Her vision returned enough for her to see the space station. A hole six feet across was visible in the outer hull. Various aspects of debris floated throughout the area beyond the broken hull. A crew of androids were already working to seal the break, tethered to the outside claps to keep from floating away. Like Xavier, each wore a protective shield to prevent them from freezing.

"Mary," Jenny thought.

"Don't worry, Jenny," Xavier thought back. "Mary is fine. The biosphere suffered no damage. They didn't even know anything had happened. You concern yourself with getting better. You know Renn is nothing without you." Jenny weakly squeezed his shoulder. Xavier realized how close they had come to losing her. "Now, why don't you shut down for a while and conserve the energy you still have? You'll be better when you wake up, and Renn will be at your side."

———————

"Renn, wake up," Glogg said as he lightly shook his friend's shoulder. "Master Kim is here, hopefully with some answers."

"Any update on Jenny?"

"Not since Xavier's report two hours ago. I'm sure if anything changes, he'll let you know. Remember, she must stay offline for at least twelve hours so her system can repair any damage caused by her expulsion."

"Why did I ever let her go?"

"Because you are a Captain and knew it was the right thing to do. Jenny was the only one who could safely get to Mary. If you had gone, there would have been no bringing you back. You'd be dead."

"And if I died, who would take over your command when you retire?"

"Still not funny," Glogg snickered. "And I said you can't die for six months. That's all. Six months." Glogg raised his hand when Master Kim entered the room in his spacesuit to signal where they were. He waited for the engineer to remove his suit before asking the question, burning in their minds. "What in the hell happened?"

"You first," Master Kim said, looking directly at Renn. "How's Jenn?

"Offline, recuperating. How's the ship?"

"It could have been worse," Master Kim said. We've had two ruptures: the first at O-fourteen hundred in Engine Room Fifteen and a second at O-fourteen and thirty hundred in a corridor above the

Habitat Sphere. The rupture in Engine Room Fifteen appears to have resulted from various circuit malfunctions. The wall outside the sphere collapsed because of a weakened structure in the engine room."

"But the station was built to withstand such ruptures," Glogg stated. "Why didn't the reinforcement program activate and secure the wall the moment it fractured?"

"That, Head Commander, my team is still working on," Master Kim said. "Glogg, there is the possibility this space station suffered some damage from sitting inside the moon for so long."

"But we checked her out completely."

"And why now? Why almost five years into our voyage?" Renn asked.

"Maybe the vibrations from folding space so many times caused a cascade effect," Master Kim replied.

"Are you saying more of these openings may occur?"

"That I cannot say."

"Is it safe to continue our voyage?

"I don't know that answer either. Repairs will take at least six weeks. After that, we'll need to re-assess our progress speed."

"If we can't fold space, how long to reach New Earth?" Renn asked.

"I did the math before I came," Master Kim said. "If we can't fold, it will take two hundred and eighteen years."

"Two hundred and eighteen?" Renn repeated.

"And that's if there are no more problems. If we encounter difficulties, we must add another hundred years to that number."

"In three hundred years, the current human inhabitants on board will be dead," Glogg said. "As will many of the other life forms. We must notify the ISC of what has happened and ask for another station to make the journey."

"Unfortunately, we still have no external communication— only internal. And that's mostly thanks to our androids' ability to talk with each other telepathically. The engine room rupture destroyed two-thirds of our outer communication system. It will take months to repair it if we can at all."

"So, we're dead in the water, with no way to go forward or call for help," Glogg sighed.

"At the moment, that is our plight, Sir."

"How long before we can leave this biosphere?" Renn asked, already getting claustrophobic in the cramped quarters.

"Five to fourteen days. It will depend on what other weaknesses we find. I can't guarantee the integrity of the station. We must seal both openings and perform an inch-by-inch inspection both inside and out. Once this is completed, I can give you a more accurate timeframe."

"Outside?"

"The second rift began outside, so we didn't detect it before it happened. From what I deduce, it is possible that the outside rapture was independent of the inside one."

"Independent? Are you sure?"

"It's only a summation. I need time to discover the truth and make this station safe," Master Kim said.

"Well, I know one thing," Glogg said as he walked around in a tight circle. "We can't stay cooped up like this for five more hours, let alone five more days. Is it possible to fortify the living residences so some of us can relocate there? Perhaps erect a force-field around decks 2 B through 3F?" We can double and triple up the families."

"My crew is spread out pretty thin. As I stated before, our priority is to restrengthen the hull and make the station space-worthy."

"What if we get you some volunteers?" Renn asked.

"What do you have in mind?" Glogg was curious about Renn's crazy plan.

Renn looked at Ron. Jeremy, and the other two young men sitting on the bench. "You asked what to do with these four. Let's put them to work erecting the force fields." Glogg gave a skeptical look. "It will keep them out of trouble."

"It's too dangerous a job," Glogg stated. "I can't take a chance on another wall opening."

"A few hours ago, you were trying to decide whether or not to execute them," Renn laughed. "Now you're afraid the job's too dangerous?"

"That's different. Besides, I never said I was going to terminate them."

"You kind of did," Ron quietly so no one would hear.

"There are a few airsuits in storage," Master Kim said. "They should fit them. Erecting a force field isn't arduous work. I don't have the men to spare to work on it. If they concentrate on the inside quarters, they won't have to go outside at all. And I'm sure Renn would be willing to supervise them."

"Me? Ah, well, I guess I could."

"Great. I'll get you the diagrams and suits right away. Is there anything else you need?"

"Someone who knows how to read the damn engineering blueprints would be helpful," Renn said. Everyone laughed.

"Excuse me," Jeremy said as he walked up. "Grandfather, Mom wants to know if you know anything about Mary. Is she all right? Jeremy walked up and said, "Grandfather, Mom wants to know if you know anything about Mary. Is she all right? When will she join us?"

"Tell your mom Mary is fine," Renn replied. "I'll be there to fill her in on what's happening as soon as I'm done. Now, Master Kim, back to my question. Whom can you spare to read those diagrams?"

"What kind of diagrams?" Jeremy asked.

"I'm sorry. Were you invited to this conversation?" Master Kim asked.

"Maybe he knows someone who can read engineering drawings," Glogg stated. "Do you know anyone, Jeremy?"

"I can some. Xavier taught me when we started designing the new flier. But I learned how to decipher and record them, thanks to Ronald. Believe it or not, he majored in engineering and was an A+ student.

"Ronald?"

"He covers it up, but he's brilliant."

"Please tell Ronald I have a job for him," Glogg stated. "Your grandfather will momentarily explain the mission to you and the rest."

"The rest of us?" Jeremy asked. "What do you mean by 'the rest of us'?"

"Glogg has determined your punishment," Renn chuckled. Jeremy, since you have solved our first problem, perhaps your brilliant mind can help with the second problem. We can't leave this area until we fortify the station, which will leave over sixteen hundred individuals smashed together in this biosphere. Can you think of anywhere we can spread out while remaining safe until the repairs are completed?

Jeremy looked at those before him with amusement and confusion. "Are you serious?" The others waited for further explanation. "You've lived in this sphere for centuries and don't know what you have?"

"Perhaps you would enlighten us?" Glogg said, now very intrigued.

"The flight hangar. It has to be compression-proof for the fliers to leave and enter. It's a biosphere set up for ships. And with most of them destroyed in the battle." Jeremy stopped when tears filled Glogg's eyes. How could he have been so insensitive? He knew that even after almost five years, Glogg had trouble dealing with his sons' deaths. "I mean, there's a lot of space in the hangar. It could easily accommodate a thousand individuals."

"He's right," Renn laughed. "We must all be getting too old if we didn't realize that."

Chapter 4: A WORRIED MOTHER

"Stop telling me there's no way to reach Mary?" Sarina yelled. "There has to be a way somehow."

"There isn't. It's way too dangerous," Renn replied. "Until they seal the holes and strengthen the structure, we don't dare let anyone go anywhere. Another rift could split the ship apart."

"It's that unstable?" Steven asked.

"It could be. Master Kim is still evaluating the extent of the damage."

"If it's that dangerous, why are you sentencing Jeremy and the others to work in the living quarters?" Sarina asked. "Why are you putting their lives in danger?"

"Master Kim assured me that part of the ship is stable enough to work in. And if something happens, they'll be in airsuits and tethered. In case of another breach, they would survive," Renn replied. "And it's not a sentencing."

"It's Glogg's judgment for eating the chicken and starting the fire," Sarina said, her eyes glaring. "I'd call that a sentence."

Renn decided to ignore his daughter's comment. The young men were the logical choice. "As for Mary, I've told you several times that the Habitat Sphere is one of the safest places to be. It has its own air supply and power system and can withstand pressurization, depressurization, and radiation."

"If they're so safe, use one of those damn pressurization suits and bring May here."

"I talked with Mary just before I came. She told me the same thing she said she told you earlier. She wants to remain where she is. The duck eggs will hatch today or tomorrow, and she doesn't want to miss their emergence."

"The ducklings can come too."

Stephen looked around at the multitude of beings in the hangar. "I think little ducklings would have little chance in this menagerie. They are safe where they are, just like Mary."

"Give me a suit, and I'll go and stay with her," Sarina demanded.

"We need the suits to work in the living quarters," Renn said for the third time. "I have none to spare."

"You can't tell me that there is not one more suit I could use in this entire spaceship?"

"Sarina, I love you dearly. But I don't have time to deal with your nonsense or your paranoia." Renn watched as a vein on the side of his daughter's face bulged with blood. He reached up and gently touched it. "Your mother's vein used to do the same thing when she was mad at me. You are so much like her. But as I said, I don't have time to argue. You can converse with Mary over the intercom. She is staying where she is, and you are staying where you are. Accept it. Jeremy, if you are ready, we will pick Harry, Ron, and Tobias up on the way out." Renn turned and walked away.

"I won't leave my daughter there," Sarina yelled as she followed her father.

Steven grabbed her arm. "Stop, Sarina. Your father is in charge, not you. You must abide by his and Glogg's decisions. What's gotten into you? This isn't like you."

Tears filled Sarina's eyes, but she kept them from trickling down her cheeks. "I'm scared, Steven. For the first time, I'm uncertain of our future. The space vessel we're on is falling apart. My daughter is on the other side of the ship, and I can't get to her. The robot representation of my mother almost died and is now lying in a coma somewhere. And my father just took my oldest son to work on a dangerous assignment. And there's nothing I can do about any of it. I'm a fixer, Steven. I always have been. When you were in Afghanistan, I stepped up and took control. But I can't do that here. I don't know what to do."

Steven pulled his terrified wife into his arms. "What you can do is hold on to me. And together, we'll trust in your father and do as he asks. He would never put either Mary or Jeremy in danger. You know that."

"I cannot simply remain in this bunker and do nothing."

"And I don't expect you to. But what about doing something that you're able to do?"

"Like what?"

"What do you think about writing a book about our trip and adventure? You've been talking about it for a couple of years now. Why not start putting down your experiences on paper? Write about the ruptures and how terrifying it was and continues to be. Or describe the different alien species and what makes each one special."

Sarina wiped a tear from her eye.

"You're serious? You want me to start writing a book now?"

"Why not? Writing has always given you purpose and a sense of accomplishment. Besides, putting words on paper gives you an energy I've never seen you have before. Plus, it will take your mind off Mary and Jeremy." Steven leaned over and kissed his wife's cheek. "Why don't you at least try?"

"It would be better than screaming at my dad every five minutes." A sheepish smile covered her face.

"I'm sure he'd happily agree."

"Alexander, please remove the prisoners' handcuffs," Renn instructed the security droid upon reaching the three prisoners. It's time for them and Jeremy to suit up and get to work."

"Are you sure this is safe, Captain Tensley?" Harry asked.

Renn could see his hands were shaking slightly. "I assure you, Mr. Wells, that you will be in no danger. Jeremy's presence alone should convince you I am not putting you in danger."

"But what if there's another breach?"

"You will always be in spacesuits and tethered to the ship. If a breach occurs, and I assure you it won't, you will be safe until a rescue crew can reach you."

"That doesn't sound very assuring, Grandfather," Jeremy said.

Renn stopped and faced the four. "I'm not going to lie to you guys. The fact is, there is a degree of danger involved in this endeavor. But our crew is spread pretty thin at the moment. They are dealing with two major apertures and a crap load of repairs. We need your help. We cannot remain cooped up here, so it is imperative that we make some of the living quarters habitable. In return for your help, Head Commander Glogg has agreed to consider your crime paid in full. So, the choice is yours. You can help us out or return to your handcuffs and await execution for your crimes."

"Tobias and Jeremy shouldn't be put in danger because of what Harry and I did," Ron stated. "Why can't they go back to their cell and stay safe?"

"Because two people can't do the job. I need all of you. So, it's all or none."

Jeremy clasped Ron on the shoulder. "Thanks, Ron, but I was part of the crime, too. And it beats sitting in that make-shift jail cell."

"Looks like you have helpers," Ron somberly said.

"If you would follow me, gentlemen." Renn led the four to a small room at the far end of the hanger. Inside hung eight airsuits. "Welcome to your new clothing. Pick one and put it on."

"These look pretty old," Ron said as he held one up. "And heavy as hell."

"Dusty, too," Harry added. "When were these used last?"

"Not in my lifetime," Renn answered. "But I assure you they are functional and will keep you safe."

"You mean if we get blasted into space," Tobias declared.

"We can't get sucked out into space," Jeremy replied. "There's too much ship between us and space. But the area could depressurize, and we'd be squashed like a bug."

"Is that true, Captain Tensley?" Tobias asked.

"Only if you're standing against the west wall," said an unfamiliar voice. The group turned and saw six humans standing outside the room.

"How will I know which one is the west wall?" Tobias questioned.

"He's joking, Tobias," Renn said. "You'll be fine. Can I help you, gentlemen?"

"Captain, my name is Cornelius Waterford. My friends and I would like to help reinforce the living quarters."

"Do you have any engineering experience?" Renn asked, surprised by the human's request.

"On Earth, we all worked as construction workers. I designed the new Trade Center in Los Angeles a year before we left. Sam here has designed buildings around the world."

"If you have that much experience, why aren't you on Master Kim's team?" Renn inquired.

"We volunteered when we first arrived here, but no one ever got back to us. We've been working various jobs around the station. We'd love the chance to do some real work."

"Can you work in a spacesuit?"

"We won't know until we try, but I see no reason we can't. It can't be much heavier than the packs we used to carry when working on tall skyscrapers back home or climbing Mt. Everest."

"You climbed Mt. Everest?" Jeremy's eyes opened wide.

"We all did."

Renn extended his hand. "Welcome aboard, Mr. Waterford. I'll have someone bring up five more suits immediately. Once you're suited up, one of the androids will bring you to our location."

"May I quickly examine the blueprints before you depart?" Cornelius inquired. Seeing no issue with a brief delay, Renn retrieved the blueprints from his pack. He unfolded a table from the wall and spread the diagrams upon it. Cornelius and Sam scrutinized them intently, conversing in hushed tones. Cornelius drew a red circle around a section of the blueprint. "See this wall here? It's a principal load-bearing wall. The two openings might have affected the station's stability and put the entire ship at risk. My team and I should inspect it before you proceed with any actions. Even minor acts, such as removing a screw or activating a light switch, could lead to severe repercussions."

The seriousness in the strangers' eyes convinced Renn of his truth. "I concede to your expertise. We'll wait for you."

"Is there a way to get prints of the entire station? To make an accurate assessment, we must see how all the walls connect, where other load-bearing joints are, and how the electrical system is constructed."

"You can do that in a few minutes?" Jeremy asked.

"No," Cornelius smiled. "To make a complete and accurate assessment would take two days."

"Shouldn't we postpone starting the job until the assessment is completely done?" Tobias asked.

Renn noticed the trembling in Harry's hands intensify. Cornelius' words had unnerved him and the others, even unnerving him a bit.

"We need this job down as soon as possible, but it must be done safely and correctly," Renn stated. "You have your two days. Meet me in section 4-C located in the corner of the hangar at 0-nine fifteen. I'll have the required blueprints for you to inspect."

"It's a date."

"Guess it's back into holding for the day, boys," Renn announced to the three parolees.

"Do we have to?" Harry asked. "I'm so tired of sitting in that room doing nothing."

"At least it's keeping you out of trouble," Renn replied. "I don't have anyone who can watch you three."

"What kind of trouble can we get into here?" Ron asked.

"I don't know, but I'm sure you'd think of something."

"If you have no objections, Captain, we'll take the four with us," Cornelius stated. "I heard Mr. Reau is good at blueprints. I am sure he and the others can help."

"Are you sure you know what you're getting yourself into?" Renn asked, pointing to Tobias, Ron, and Harry. "These three are known for getting into trouble. They can be a handful. And as for my grandson, let's just say he's had his share of infractions."

"I'm aware of Mr. Reau and his friends' shenanigans. I've been the recipient of two or three myself. And when he's not getting into trouble, Harry dates my middle daughter. We'll keep a good eye on them. Plus, it will give us a chance to work together."

"They're all yours."

"I thought I might find you here," Glogg said as he entered the temporary medical unit in the small biosphere. Renn was sitting beside Jenny's gurney. Glogg looked down at the lifeless android's body. Her skin looked cold, artificial, lifeless. Did Renn notice the change? Probably not. "How's she doing?"

"Dr. Chi said her circuits have completed their repair. He will slowly warm up her blood supply so her body will return to normal. If all goes well, he should be able to wake her up sometime tomorrow."

"Did she suffer any damage?"

"Not that he could tell. All her relays checked out fine, and her heart was functioning within parameters. Once she's awake, he can evaluate her subroutines to see if they function normally." Renn sighed deeply. "He doesn't know if her positronic brain suffered any damage when she froze out there."

"I thought she has a layer of dyrillium beneath her skin layer to prevent her circuits and organs from ever being damaged because of extreme heat or cold."

"She does. But for some reason, her defenses didn't kick in like they were supposed to. Dr. Chi speculates that whatever caused the wall to rupture may have also affected her."

"But what could affect both Jenny and the station?"

"That is a mystery we must solve before it happens again. Dr. Chi notified Master Kim and Xavier of his suspicions so they could incorporate them into their investigations." Renn gave another long, drawn-out sigh. "What will I do, Glogg, if she no longer retains all of Jenny's memories? What if when she wakes up, she's not My Jenny any longer?"

"If the unthinkable happens, you will tell her those memories and make new ones together." Glogg reached into his pocket and removed a delicately blue flower. He gently placed it over Jenny's bionic heart. "A custom on my homeworld for the sick. It's a #((@*# flower. There's no translation for it in the data banks. It has healing properties. I had one sent up from the greenhouse. We used them to help those injured in the fight with the Keel."

"Did they work?"

"Yes, very effectively."

"Thank you, My Friend."

Glogg knew what loss was. First, his mate so long ago, followed by his three sons in the war. "I hear you have some new recruits on your team."

"Yeah. I was shocked when Cornelius told me about his experience. How did we not know about him and his crew?"

"When I checked their records, I discovered that their engineering abilities were documented, although hidden towards the back of the folders. This makes me wonder what else was overlooked with the newcomers.

"You're not thinking one of them might have sabotaged the station, do you?"

"That thought has crossed my mind. We never had trouble with the station before."

"But we never took her out of the moon before. She sat for what? Five thousand years? And has been folding space for over four years? That's a lot to ask for any vessel, no matter how well-built.

"I keep telling myself the same thing."

"But the fact this happened now as we draw close to our destination can't be coincidental."

"And neither of us believes in coincidences. Renn, I have a job for you. I'll attend your meeting with Cornelius and go over the schematics. You remain here with Jenny and go through the new arrivals' paperwork. See if there's anything else out of the ordinary, anything not followed up on."

"And if there is?"

"If there are more inconsistencies, the saboteur is likely one of our own and not a newcomer."

"Do you want me to bring Xavier in on this?"

"No. For the moment, it will be just between us."

"You're worried there's a saboteur on board, aren't you? I've never excluded Xavier from an investigation I was conducting before. I trust him with my life."

"As do I, but until I have more information, I do not have the luxury of trusting the androids either."

"And if the androids ARE involved somehow, Xavier would know. What about Jenny?"

"As I said, we'll wait to see what you uncover."

Chapter 5: ANSWERS AND MORE QUESTIONS

"Where's Renn?" Xavier asked upon entering the meeting.

"I told him to remain with Jenny," Glogg said as he sat. "Dr. Chi believed his presence might stimulate Jenny's positronic brain."

"How's she doing?"

"Unknown. We won't know if there was any damage to Jenny's circuits until she wakes up." Glogg paused for a moment, thinking. "She was dang lucky you were in the vicinity and were able to rescue her. Why were you in that area? You were supposed to be on the other end of the station critiquing the damage of the first breach."

"We picked up a strange vibration in the broken framework," Xavier answered. I followed it and surmised it originated from outside the habitat, so I went to investigate."

"It's good that you did, or our friend would have lost his Jenny." Glogg scrutinized the artificial life form with his large, black eyes. Was Xavier telling the truth? Robots couldn't lie, but something didn't seem right. Could Xavier be behind the catastrophe? "Did you determine what caused the vibration or what it was?"

"No. When the rupture occurred, the affected material jettisoned into space. If I wanted a reason for the explosion, I needed samples to examine. I went outside to retrieve the fragments and that's when I saw Jenny floating outside the station. It was clear that she was in distress. When I reached her, I pulled her to me; her body was so cold. As I held her closer I detected the same vibrations in her that I witnessed in the beached wall."

"In her?"

"Although her outsides would have frozen over due to the extreme cold, her inner circuits should not have been affected. Yet they were. Whatever destroyed the station walls also tried to attack Jenny."

"Master Kim and Dr. Chi voiced the same possibility. Do you have any idea what it was or why it attacked Jenny? Have any of the other androids shown signs of infection?"

"I do not know why Jenny was affected. And no other androids have shown signs of contamination. Their internal alarms would have notified me immediately."

"Why didn't Jenny's?"

"As you know, Jenny is unique and one of a kind. Even though I can speak with her telepathically, I am not privy to her internal controls."

"Is it possible some alien organisms or bacteria are attacking the station?"

"Again, I do not have sufficient data to answer. I know repairs were made on that station section a decade ago. Due to the unavailability of the original giizerite used to build the station, we opted for tilithium. The area of the first breach also had some minor reinforcement done with tilithium."

"But that wouldn't explain what happened to Jenny," Glogg said. "Tilithium is not used in the manufacturing of synthetic life forms."

"That is normally true. However, Jenny is unique. She was built specifically for Renn. I talked with Dr. Chi, who confirmed that tilithium was used in Jenny's manufacturing. It is the first layer of her positronic matrix." Xavier paused. "I believe, Sir, they are ready to begin the meeting."

Glogg looked up and noticed everyone was looking at him, waiting for him to say something. He cleared his throat and stood. "Captain Renn is attending to other matters, so I will attend in his place. Mr. Waterford, thank you for your help. Please proceed."

Cornelius brought the schematics of the remodeling area up on the screen. "As you can see, strengthening the outside circumference at these junctions will be simple. I estimate it should take five days to complete the process. However, my team and I discovered one flaw." The computer displayed an area outside of Glogg's family quarters. "We picked up unusual vibrations outside of Head Commander Clog's quarters. Specifically, along the door frame to the entrance of his home."

"A few years ago, the outside door malfunctioned. It wouldn't close. Maintenance installed a new door."

Xavier stood. "Computer, Captain Xavier, designation 4C-8Z-Security captain. Access repair records of living quarters 1A, corridor A, level 2B."

"Accessing," announced a female voice.

"What alloys were used in the construction?"

"Seventy percent reprocessed giizerite, twelve percent aluminum, eight percent bio-carbon formitite, six percent quixrat, two percent iron, two percent tilithium."

"Computer, how long has tilithium been used to repair the station?"

"Tilithium was first used one thousand four hundred and twelve years ago."

"Computer, Glogg, Commander of Freedom Station, authorization 1A-1B-1A-comply. What portion of the station did they repair using the alloy tilithium?

"Calculating," came the feminine voice. "Approximately sixty-three percent of the station contains tilithium. The heaviest concentrates are the outside wall opposite Engine Room 15 and the walls along corridor 4B, panels 4-15 through 4-36."

"Computer, is there any indication that any tilithium was used on the biospheres?" Xavier asked.

"No, although section 3-y of the life incubation sphere is scheduled to receive an upgrade in two days."

"Cancel that assignment," Glogg shouted. "Authorization 1A-1B-1A."

"Does the main hangar contain any tilithium?" Xavier asked.

"Checking." Silence filled the area as they awaited the computer's answer. "I can find no record of tilithium being used in the main hangar."

"Computer, did someone alter your records?" Xavier asked.

"You think the records could have been changed?" Glogg inquired.

"Someone could have altered records to cover the culprit's tracks."

"There is no way to alter my records."

"I hope that's true," Glogg said. "Who authorized the original introduction of tilithium in building materials?"

"Then Lieutenant Juaquin authorized the change."

"Computer, do you know why the change was made?"

"There was a lack of resources. Tilithium was the only alloy available to substitute for the missing giizerite. When more favorable alloys became available, the formula was not corrected."

"Computer, is there a way to neutralize the tilithium?"

"No."

"And you're sure Juaquin authorized the switch to tilithium?" Renn asked Glogg, shocked at the possible ramifications of this new information.

"Positive. I checked it out myself. But more troubling than the fact that it was used is that it does not show on the original orders for my door. You know me; I keep everything, and thankfully, I kept the repair slip the crew had given me."

"You mean it was omitted?"

"No, I mean the computer log was altered. The other alloys' percentages were changed to accommodate the missing tilithium."

"Who signed the final log?"

"Captain Juaquin."

Renn didn't like where this was headed. He trusted Juaquin as much as he did Xavier. "You know, it's possible Juaquin did not know of the discrepancy."

"I have considered that."

"What do we do now?"

"Monitor Juaquin and the robots under his command," Glogg said. "Keep Xavier in the dark about what we suspect."

"And what do we suspect?"

"That one or more of the robots is responsible for these ruptures and breakdowns, intentionally or unintentionally. "

"Could some embers from Ron's illegal fire have gotten into the ventilation shaft and caused the incidents?"

"Although unlikely, it is a possibility," Glogg said. I sent Xavier into the control shafts to see if there were any signs of burning on the walls. I should have his report within the hour."

"Have they located Harry or that lost pig yet?"

"A few sightings of Peaches. But she was too fast for the guards to catch him."

"Who is Peaches?" Renn asked.

"That's what the Habitat crew named her when she came out of cryogenics. Apparently, because she has a peachy skin color," Xaver replied.

"And Harry?"

"We've had no sign of him on any of the surveillance cameras. There is a possibility that he got sucked out in one of the breaches or asphyxiated down some obscure hallway we haven't checked yet. What did you find out in your search?"

"Disturbing facts. Master Kim never incorporated Mr. Waterford and the others because their engineering expertise was not mentioned in the reports he received," Renn said. "Yet when you checked the original paperwork, you said their original paperwork stated they were the highest quality engineers."

"It did. Do you think someone doctored the logs, like they did with my door repair?

"Yes. And not just Mr. Waterford's or his team's. I've come across thirty-six discrepancies so far. Someone wanted to hide information about the newcomers that would benefit this ship."

"But why?"

"I have no idea."

"Who inputted the information into the computer?" Glogg held his breath, hoping the answer was not Juaquin or Xavier."

"Robot number RP-18. "

"RB-18 was on GiiJew's ship. He was third in command."

"Yep, which means he took the secret of why he altered the logs to his grave."

After Mr. Waterford and his team certified the living area's safety, Jeremy, Ronald, Tobias, and Henry began working on the living quarters on levels 2B through 3F. The young men and the construction crew found working in the spacesuits cumbersome and tiring. The suits were heavy, and the circulation inside was poor. Everyone had trouble holding their tools through the thick gloves. After only two hours, the crew had to take a half-hour rest.

Twelve minutes into the break, Glogg walked down the hallway outside the confinement area. "Commander Glogg, it is not safe to be down here without a suit," Cornelius said.

"I promised Una I would retrieve her favorite stuffed toy," Glogg responded. "Since your team deemed this area safe enough to work inside, I thought I'd sneak in and retrieve her Grubby and a few things I needed."

"That may be, Commander, but it's still unsafe around here without a spacesuit."

"I'm afraid they don't make them big enough to accommodate my stature. Besides, I'll be in and out within minutes. I assure you it's okay."

"Did Xavier okay this?"

'Let's say it's our little secret," Glogg whispered. "No reason to worry Xavier." Cornelius gave Glogg an odd look. Xavier was head of security. He knew everything, sometimes even before you did something. He had an uncanny way of anticipating what people were going to do. Before Cornelius could object again, Glogg stepped around the human and swiftly slipped through the plastic petition, down the hallway, and into his apartment. The human hoped nothing would happen to the Commander. If it did, there would be hell to be paid.

Glogg stood in the foyer of his living quarters, allowing his large oval eyes to adjust to the dim lighting. After learning about tilithium, he was afraid to raise the lights. There was no sense in pressing his luck. Using his hands, he carefully felt his way into the den.

"Computer. Top security clearance Glogg, sequence 1-A, 1-B, 1-AB. Code (#*W@&(*W&." For the first time, Glogg was happy the intelligent robots could not decipher the Caelifera clicks. The last part of his security clearance ensured that no one, not even Xavier, would have access to what he was about to do.

"Computer, access Captain Xavier's files, intelligent life form RZ-47G, number 18345."

"Accessing. File available."

"Have there been any modifications in this model?"

"There was a complete upgrade in all RZ-47Gs two thousand years ago. No additional modifications have been made since."

"Computer, was the alloy tilithium used in the upgrade?"

"Accessing. Accessing. That information is not available."

"Why not?

"The logs from that period have been erased."

"By whom?

"Unknown."

"Computer, have any intelligent life forms had repairs or alternations since that time?"

"Jenny Spalling underwent restoration two days ago."

"Besides her."

There was a brief pause as the computer checked her database. "Yes. RZ-47G unit number 1922, known as Juaquin, suffered damage while trying to secure a mother bear and her cubs five hundred and six years ago this September 18th.:

Glogg remembered that incident. Although indestructible, that angry mother bear had almost torn Juaquin to pieces. He had extensive repairs. "Computer, was tilithium used in Juaquin's repairs?"

"The database shows no such alloy used." Glogg breathed a sigh. "But my secret database indicates tilithium was used in fifty-three percent of his repairs."

A chill ran down Glogg's spine. "Computer, why do you possess a secret database? And who has access to it?"

"After my data logs concerning the tilithium in the robotics repairs were erased, I created a separate log of all events. The only people who can access it are the Head Commander and me."

"When were you planning on telling me about this secret unit?"

"I just did."

"Computer, is it possible the records showing RZ-47G robot Juaquin received tilithium repairs were erased before you could store them in your new file?"

"No. I created the new database the moment an erasure was detected, and I stored all events since that date instantaneously in my new memory. Nothing can be deleted or not recorded."

"Computer, is there any way Captain Xavier can access or change this database?"

"No. Only the Head Commander has access. And no one, not even I, can erase data." Glogg had to make sure Xavier never became Head Commander, not even for a second.

"Computer, is there any way to identify if RZ-23G robot Xavier has received tilithium repairs or upgrades?"

"RZ-23G has received no tilithium since creating my new database. However, before that time, I cannot attest to. It is possible those recordings were deleted."

"But wouldn't you have detected the erasure?"

"Unknown."

"Why would you detect the erasure on RZ-47G and not RX-23G?"

"Unknown,"

"Computer, can an android lie?"

"Yes."

"Intentionally?"

"Yes, thanks to the new programming."

"Can an android override his programming?"

"Yes."

"Computer, can an android ignore his programming and Head Commander's orders and arrive at an independent decision that prompts an independent action."

"Yes."

"Computer, can an android go against his primary directive and end the inhabitants' lives aboard this station?"

"Yes."

Glogg grabbed the end of the desk to prevent himself from collapsing. The ramifications of what he had just heard were unbelievable, and the possible outcomes multiplied exponentially.

"Commander Glogg, I have received reports that you are in your living quarters without the proper precautionary gear." Xavier's voice boomed over the comm link, making Glogg jump. "I must insist you vacate the area immediately."

"I was just on my way out," he replied. "I promised Una I'd get her Grubby." He turned to hurry to her room to retrieve his excuse for being there when he heard a sound.

"Hello? Is someone there?" Silence. "You're getting paranoid, Glogg. No one heard your conversation with the computer." He quickly felt his way to Una's room in the dark and retrieved the stuffed glindersnorf from her bedroom. Retracing his steps, he turned the corner and observed that the lights in his den were slightly elevated. Had there been another malfunction? Or had he raised the lights without realizing it? A sudden movement through the glass window confirmed it was no malfunction. He pressed the silent alarm on his coat to alert Xavier that he needed security.

"Whose there? Announce yourself. I've alerted Security and their on their way."

Advancing Glogg shielded his eyes with his hand to diminish some of the lights' glare. He stared at his desk. Lying there, with a large knife stuck through its heart, was the missing Peaches. Blood was oozing out of the dying animal and dripping over the desk edge onto the floor. Glogg was sure it hadn't been there when he went into his daughter's bedroom.

"Is that pig's fate what you had planned for us for eating that stupid chicken?" Harry asked as he stepped out of the shadows with an assault gun aimed at Glogg's heart.

"Harry, I'm glad to see you," Glogg calmly said, hoping to stall until Xavier came bursting through the door. "We feared you were killed in the explosions. Everyone will be delighted to hear you are alive." Glogg slowly brought up his communicator.

"Press it, and I'll blow your fricking head off," Harry shouted.

The last few days had taken a toll on Harry. He was thin, and his clothes were tattered, dirty, and stained with blood.

"You look like you could use something good to eat. Why don't we go to the mess hall and get you something?"

"Why? How could you sentence him to death for eating a chicken and building a small fire? It wasn't his fault. I didn't know that little fire would cause any harm to the station."

"So, you were the one who built the fire. Mr. Reau never told us which one of you did."

"He didn't tell you because he was my friend. Without knowing the truth, you sentenced him to death."

"No, Harry, Ronald's okay. He's right outside in the hallway. I can get him for you."

"Move, and I'll kill you."

"Glogg, you had best come out. Xavier is on his way, and he's not too happy," Cornelius yelled into the apartment.

"Be right there. Can you send Ronald in?"

"I don't think that's a good idea," Cornelius said as he drew closer to the den. He stopped upon seeing Harry holding a weapon. "Right away." He disappeared. Moments later, Ron stepped into the room. He removed his helmet so Harry could see it was him.

"Hey there, Harry. I've been worried sick about you," Ron calmly stated. I'm working with this guy named Cornelius to fortify this part of the station. We could use another good helper. Want to get your hands dirty?"

"Ron, is that you? Glogg didn't kill you?"

"No, but I'm not going to be able to say the same about you if you don't put that gun down. Xavier won't ask questions before firing."

"No, no, no. This isn't real." Harry pounded his head with his free hand. "You're not here. Glogg killed you."

"No, man, I'm alive and well." Ron took a step forward.

Harry turned the gun towards Ron. "No, you're not real."

"I'm real, Sport. Hey, remember when we hooked up with those cheerleaders from Scott's High? No figment would know that?"

"Yes, it would because the imposter knows everything I do."

"Harry, you've only got seconds before Xavier bursts through the door and kills you. Put the gun down now." Seeing Harry hesitate, Ron rushed forward.

"No, Harry, don't shoot," Glogg shouted as he leapt in front of Ron as Harry fired his weapon. Glogg screamed and fell to the floor, his left shoulder a mass of bone and blood.

The security android entered the room, his gun drawn, just as Glogg screamed out in pain. Xavier immediately fired, hitting the young human in the chest. Harry's eyes widened in horror as a circle of light appeared in the middle of his chest. The glow grew until it encompassed Harry's entire body. Harry's shrieked, his cries of unimaginable pain echoed throughout the room, followed by complete silence. A few remaining ashes slowly drifted down to the floor.

"You killed him," Ron shouted as he charged the android. Reacting to the new threat, Xavier aimed his gun and fired. The streak of death zoomed past Ronald's head as Jeremy grabbed his friend's spacesuit and pulled him to the floor.

"Stop it, or he'll kill you too."

"You son-of-a-bitch," Ronald screamed, trying to break Jeremy's hold and claw his way to the standing android. "Couldn't you see he was out of his head?"

Xavier adjusted his setting and aimed at the two humans.

"Xavier, stand down," Glogg screamed. "I order you to cease. DO NOT fire on either Ron or Jeremy." Xavier did not divert his attention from the two young males, his finger poised on the trigger.

The cumbersomeness of their suits made it impossible for Jeremy to keep his hold. Ron freed his leg, pulled it towards his body, and kicked Jeremy in the stomach. Jeremy moaned and curled up in pain. Ron bolted to his feet and charged the android. Xavier fired.

"Medical assistance needed in the Head Commander's apartment immediately," Cornelius yelled into his mike. "Hello? Is anyone there? Damn, communications must be down again."

"Xavier to A-1 security grid," the android said as he rushed to the injured Glogg. Please send medical help to Glogg's living quarters. Head Commander Glogg was seriously injured. One human is unconscious, and another human is injured. Both need transporting to a holding cell. Send someone to notify Renn of the incident."

"Hold on, Sir. Help is on the way." Xavier examined Glogg's wound. It wasn't good. He noted that most of Glogg's left shoulder and upper arm were blasted away. A large pool of blood was pooling beneath the Head Commander's body. "This is going to hurt, Glogg." Xavier lifted his shirt and opened a small panel on his right side. He removed a small packet of white powder. Using his teeth, he ripped the packet open and poured the powder onto the mangled shoulder. Glogg screamed as the powder hardened, encasing the wound. Xavier grabbed a nearby blanket and wrapped it around Glogg's. He removed a belt from around his waist and tied it around the towel and across Glogg's chest." That should stop the bleeding until I get you to the infirmary."

"Grubby," Glogg whispered, trying to reach out with his other hand.

Cornelius walked over and picked an odd-looking stuffed animal off the floor. "It's Una's stuffed animal that he came to get. I'll make sure she gets it."

Chapter 6: A MISSING ANDROID

"Now remember, her memory might be a little foggy at first," Dr. Chi cautioned as he brought Jenny online. "Don't press her. Let her tell you by her actions what she remembers and doesn't."

"I'll try," Renn said. He wondered how much of the real Jenny's memories his Jenny maintained. All? None? A portion? His heart was pounding, and beads of sweat appeared on his forehead.

"Dr. Chi, you're needed in medical right away," said an orderly who burst into the room. "Commander Glogg was critically wounded."

"What do you mean, wounded? How?" shouted Renn. Dr. Chi turned and proceeded toward the exit. "Doc, what about Jenny? You can't leave."

"I'm afraid there's nothing either of us can do," Dr. Chi replied. "She's going to wake up whether I'm here or not. You're the one who needs to stay with her. She'll want to see you when she wakes up, not me. Plus, a Head Commander's life is more valuable than an AI's life." With that, he left the room, leaving the speaker alone with the patient.

"Someone tell me what in the hell is going on?" Renn shouted. He jumped to his feet and grabbed his communicator, punching in his priority code. "Xavier, come in." There was no response. "Xavier, can you hear me?" Silence. "Can anyone hear me? I need an update NOW." No response came. Renn threw the device onto the floor, smashing it into pieces. "Useless piece of shit."

"Dad," came Sarina's voice as she ran into the room. "Have you heard? Harry shot Glogg."

"Harry? Where did he come from?"

"He's been hiding in Glogg's apartment, which is why no one could find him. Glogg went there to get Una's stuff Grubby and found Harry."

Renn looked at the door. "Where's Steven?"

"Ron and Jeremy got arrested again. Steven went to see what he could find out since communications aren't working again."

"Arrested? For what?"

"I don't know.

"What about Harry?"

Sarina's eyes filled with tears. "Xavier killed him."

Of course he did. Xavier's programming dictated that he eliminate the threat immediately. Stupid kid! How often did he warn those guys about the police robots' charge over them in aggression cases? They had complete control, control that could not be revoked.

"Do you know how bad Glogg is?" Renn asked.

"On the way in here, I overheard one of the medical personnel say they don't think he'll make it."

Renn sensed a slight touch on his hand. He looked down to observe Jenny awake and smiling at him. "Go. You are the second in command. Your place is with your Commander."

"Jenny, you're awake!" Renn said, taking her into his arms. "I thought I lost you. I was so scared."

"I'm all right," Jenny said. "You need to see how bad Glogg is."

"I can't leave you. We still don't know if you suffered any damage. What if something happens again?"

"I'll stay with her, Dad," Sarina said. "If something happens, I'll send someone for you. Besides, he's just down the hallway. You'll still be close."

"Renn, I promise you my systems are functioning perfectly." Doubt filled Renn's eyes. "I am missing memory algorithms from the past few days, but everything else is operating at peak performance. Trust me. You must go to Glogg. Xavier must not take over command, not even for a few minutes."

Renn tilted his head to the side and looked at Jenny. "Why do you say that? Why can't Xavier take over command? Is there something about Xavier I should know? Is he behind these beaches?"

"I don't know. All I know is that he must not become Head Commander. Not now." Jenny smiled. "Go. I'll be here when you return."

Renn wrestled with his conscience. Should he go? Should he stay? What if Jenny malfunctioned, or worse yet, stopped operating, and he wasn't there? He'd never forgive himself.

"Go." Jenny gave him a slight push.

Kissing Jenny on the forehead, Renn bolted from the room. He ran down the hallway to the central medical unit.

"I'm coming, Old Friend. Stay alive until I get there."

———————

"You're getting old," Xavier said upon seeing Renn burst through the door. Unable to speak, Renn's chest moved up and down as he sucked in mouthfuls of air. He held onto the door frame to keep from collapsing. "I need to get you back into a daily exercise regimen."

Renn didn't have to ask where his friend was. From behind the door to his right resonated Glogg's screams. Shivers descended Renn's body with each blood-curdling sound.

"You're to go right in," Xavier said. "He's refused treatment until you got here."

"Why?"

"I do not know why. He wouldn't tell the doctors or me."

What was happening? First, Jenny said he couldn't allow Xavier to take charge. Now, Glogg won't let the doctors treat him until he arrives. What didn't he know?

Taking a deep breath and forcing a smile, Renn entered the operating room. Glogg lay on the table, countless tubes extended from his body. Glogg's left shoulder and upper arm were now a mass of charred flesh covered with thick blue blood. Shards of beige-blue bone protruded through the flesh. Renn understood why Xavier didn't hesitate to shoot Harry. Another shout would undoubtedly have killed Glogg. Hell, had he been there, he probably would have killed Harry himself.

"Thank goodness you're here," Dr. Robinson said upon seeing Renn. "This damn fool won't let me treat him until he talks with you. Won't even let me give him something for the excoriating pain he's in."

"What are you doing, my dearest friend?" Renn asked, tears filling his eyes. "Why won't you let Doctors Robinson and Chi treat you? You're hurt badly."

Glogg motioned for Renn to lean down. He didn't have the strength to make his words heard. "Don't trust them. Xavier and the others?"

"The androids?" Renn whispered.

"Record."

"Communications are still down."

"Record." Renn realized his friend wanted him to record something. He brought out his recorder, pressed the record button, and held it close to Glogg's mouth. "Command Glogg unfit for duty for medical reasons," Glogg said through clenched teeth. "Captain Renn Tensley is now acting Head Commander. Authorization 1-A, 1-B, 3-AB. Code (#*W@&(*W&." He grabbed Renn's shirt as he screamed out in pain. Somehow, through the pain and clenched teeth, he managed to say. "The computer. My den. Talk to her." Glogg became silent, and his eyes dimmed.

"No! Don't you dare die on me, Glogg." He turned towards the doctor. "Is he dead?"

"Pretty close," Dr. Robinson said. "Now, if you are finished, let us try to save what life he still has."

Sniffling, Renn wiped the constantly flowing tears from his eyes as he walked towards Xavier.

"Is he dead?"

"The docs are doing their best to keep him alive."

"Why did he wait for treatment? What was so important?"

"He wanted to transfer Head Command to me."

A slight rigidness appeared in Xavier's stature. Was he upset by Glogg giving him command? Had Xavier planned on being the next Head Commander? That didn't make sense; droids didn't have ambitions. Glogg said not to trust the androids. Not even Xavier. Why? What did Glogg discover in his den? What was hidden inside the computer? He had to get inside that room without Xavier knowing.

"Commander, I am at your service."

"What happened, Xavier?" Renn asked. "Why was Glogg in his off-limits apartment? What was Harry doing there? Why are my grandson and Ron under arrest again?"

"I discovered Glogg had returned to his living quarters to get Una's toy, although I'm not sure that was the real reason. Unbeknownst to any of us, Harry had been hiding out in his apartment. That's why we couldn't find him. Because of the need for complete secrecy, there are no monitors in the Head Commander's quarters so he can conduct necessary business."

"But there are still security devices. Why didn't they notify us that a living presence was in Glogg's quarters?"

"I do not know for sure. The security system in Glogg's and your quarters is on a separate system that operates even without station power or communications. But for some reason, they malfunctioned or were shut down."

"Shut down? By whom?"

"Unknown, Sir. I have sent Juaquin to your quarters to determine if your abode's system is also malfunctioning."

"Keep me informed."

"When I learned of Glogg's trip to his quarters, I contacted him and advised him he was to leave the premises immediately. The communications went down again, and I could not ascertain whether Glogg had departed. So, I hurried down to his abode, but I arrived too late. When I arrived, I found Harry standing behind Glogg's desk. The missing pig laid on the desk, slaughtered, his blood dripping onto the carpet."

"The pig?" Who killed the pig?"

"I think Harry did. Harry aimed his gun at Ronald, and the kid was petrified. It was evident Harry was not sane. Ron tried to talk him down because he knew I would not hesitate to end the scenario when I arrived. As I walked through the door, Ron reacted, and Harry fired. Glogg leapt in front of the boy and saved his life. I fired on Harry. When Ronald witnessed what I did, he attacked me. I fired to eliminate him, but Jeremy jumped in and knocked Ron to the floor. Not knowing what else to do, I stunned both and had them put into holding until I could sort things out."

"You fired on my grandson?" Renn shouted, startling the nurses standing nearby.

"He was not in the scene when I originally fired," Xavier said with no emotion. It was all so matter of fact with him. "I did not anticipate his move."

"And if you had? Would you still have fired?" Xavier gave no response. "ANSWER ME."

"You know my programming, Commander. I am programmed to eliminate all acts of aggression."

"Answer me, you piece of metal."

For a moment, Renn thought a glimmer of hurt appeared in Xavier's eyes. Had the androids experienced emotions? Was that the underlying problem?

"Yes," Xavier replied.

Renn stood and walked away from Xavier, his back to him. When he turned around, he held his gun in his hand. Without looking, Xavier knew the red target beam was in the middle of his forehead.

"If I decide to shoot you, are you going to kill me, Xavier?" Renn asked.

"You know your bullets cannot pierce my skin."

"Would you kill me?"

"I…" Xavier paused, his head twitching ever so slightly. "I do not know."

Why didn't Xavier know? His programming dictated an instinctive reaction – a simple affirmative should have been his immediate response. The hesitation of his reply hinted at something more profound. Could this android harbor genuine emotions, sentiments strong enough to override his programmed directives? Is that why Jenny warned him? And how did she know?

Renn lowered his weapon and returned it to its case. "You're such a piece of shit." He walked past the android and headed down the hallway.

"Where are you going, Commander?"

"To retrieve My Jenny and get my grandson out of jail," Renn yelled. "After that, I'll be on the bridge where I am needed. DO NOT be there when I arrive or, so help me, God, I WILL find a way to shut you down."

———————

Renn escorted Sarina and Jenny to a safe place inside the small biosphere. Once they were secure, he walked to the makeshift holding cells to retrieve Ron and Jeremy. He nodded to Stephen, who was standing outside the cells. Saying nothing, he bypassed the two police androids, grabbed the keys from the hook, and unlocked the door. Seeing the look on the captain's face, the police androids did not try to stop him. Renn walked directly up to Jeremy and pulled him into his arms. "You crazy, stupid kid. If you ever put yourself in front of a firing android again, so help me, I'll shoot you myself."

"I couldn't let Xavier kill Ron," Jeremy offered as an excuse. "Plus, I knew Xavier wouldn't hurt me."

"You don't know that. Xavier and I have been best friends for a hundred years, and I wouldn't even trust him not to shoot me. Never, ever try to second-guess his or any android's programming. Promise me."

"I promise," Jeremy said.

"You too, Ron," Renn said. "Promise me you will not try to second-guess an android's programming."

"But he killed Harry," Ron shouted.

"Promise me."

"He killed him in cold blood with no warning."

"Promise me."

"All right."

"All right, what? I want to hear you say it."

"I promise not to second-guess an android's programming."

"Thank you. And I am sorry for the loss of your friend. I know Harry only shot Glogg because he was scared and confused."

"How is Glogg?" Jeremy asked.

"Not good. I know that right now, none of this makes sense, and I'm not making excuses for him, but Xavier operated according to his programming parameters – to safeguard the life of his superior officer. He didn't shoot Harry out of malice or hate. He did what his circuits directed him to – save his Head Commander's life. A tragic outcome, but one driven by code rather than malice." Both boys were crying. Renn placed his arm around Jeremy. "Let's get out of here."

Renn and Stephen escorted Jeremy and Ron back to where Jenny, Sarina, and Tim waited. Sarina grabbed her son and hugged him. She next pulled Ron into the embrace. "You two are going to give me a heart attack yet. Are you okay?"

"We're fine, Mom," Jeremy said, squirming from Sarina's tight embrace.

"Did you really see Glogg get shot and Xavier kill Harry?" Tim asked. "I wish I had been there."

"No, you don't," Ron said, choking on his words.

"I think it's time to change the subject," Steven stated. "And I'm sure these two young men would like a bite to eat and rest. Let's go over to the mess area and grab a bit."

"I must get to the bridge," Renn said, taking Jenny's hand. "I seem to keep leaving you when all I want to do is to be here with you. I'm sorry I can't stay."

"I am aware of your responsibilities and am not offended by your departure."

Renn kissed Jenny goodbye and headed for the bridge. Silently he cursed Harry for incapacitating Glogg and Glogg for going to his quarters after that damn children's toy. If Glogg had stayed put like he was supposed to, Renn would be with Jenny. She needed him. And he had to know what damage she suffered. But as Glogg had told him many times, the Head Commander's place was on the bridge. Maybe being Head Commander wouldn't be as great as he thought.

The moment he stepped onto the bridge, Renn surveyed the room. Xavier was nowhere to be seen. The android had taken his advice. But the room was filled with other droids – lower-ranking ones who helped run the ship. Was there a way to shut THEM down? Were they part of a conspiracy? He was always told the police droids were invincible and could never be cycled down, but what about these droids? Was that why Glogg wanted him to talk with the computer in Glogg's abode? Had he found the secret to turning the androids off? He had to get to Glogg's office the moment he could leave the bridge.

For six hours, Glogg was in surgery. His three hearts had each stopped twice, and each time, the doctors were able to start them again. They removed the mangled flesh and tied off his shoulder's arteries and veins. Caelifera lined the medical wing's hallways, donating blood to replenish what their commander had lost, others giving slices of flesh the doctors used to repair Glogg's lower left arm. But the muscles needed for the arm to function properly were in the part of the shoulder blasted away and could not be replaced.

Renn sighed loudly. As he waited for word on Glogg, he paced the bridge, contemplating his next move. There were so many questions he had no answers for, and the answers he did have unsettled him. Plus, the space station was inoperable and had two huge holes in its outside hull. What if he couldn't repair the damage? Would their cargo of valuable flora and fauna survive?

Finally, a messenger came to the bridge to inform Renn that Glogg had survived the surgery. He was in recovery. It was still unknown if he would live. The next twenty-four hours would tell them if there was hope for their beloved Commander.

"Commander, any estimate when I will have communication?" Renn asked.

"I wish I did, Sir. That second breach took out most of our communication wiring. We're trying to reroute some of the terminals. Someone knew exactly what they were doing."

"So, you think it was intentional?"

"There is no proof either way. But I don't believe a rupture just happened to occur over our main communication relays."

The thought that the station was sabotaged sent a shiver down Renn's spine. He yawned. It had been a long, tiring day.

"Sir, there's nothing you can do here," Lucas said. "Why don't you get some rest? If you are needed, I can send someone to retrieve you."

"I am tired. And I must check on my family," Renn stated.

Renn headed towards the hangar. He needed to visit Glogg's apartment, but he was too exhausted. One doesn't think well when one is that tired. Glogg's secrets would have to wait a little longer. Besides, he needed to see how Jenny was doing.

Renn walked over to where his family was asleep on their cots. Everyone except Jenny. She was sitting on their cot, waiting for her beloved. Without a word, Renn laid down and drew Jenny into his arms, kissing her softly on the forehead. Within seconds, he was sound asleep, safe from exploding space stations, safe from angry humans, safe from dysfunctioning synthetic lifeforms. But his dreams were filled with them. He dreamt Xavier shot and killed Jeremy when he tried to save Ronald. As his grandson sunk to the floor, the killer android turned his weapon on Renn and fired.

Grasping his abdomen, he bolted up in bed. The sting of the imaginary weapon's fire filled his torso, disintegrating the molecules in his body. Sweat ran down his face, and his body trembled. Jenny opened her eyes.

"I'm sorry to wake you," he quietly announced.

"Your dreams trouble you tonight. Would you like me to make you some tea?"

"No. I think I'm going to go for a walk. See if I can tire myself out."

"Would you like me to accompany you?"

"No, you stay here and rest."

"I am an android, Renn. I do not require rest."

"Perhaps you could watch over our family." He gave her a loving smile.

"I can do that."

As he neared the exit, Renn noticed a young android named Boyd #132 walking towards him. He remembered when this android was constructed and activated. Renn was eight at the time. It was the first time he had witnessed an android's emergence. The two formed a friendship and spent many hours together. Over time, the two grew apart because of the android's duties, but Renn always kept informed of Boyd #132's doings. Was this young android capable of killing him or his family for no reason? If he found a way, could he terminate the young android? So many questions with no answers.

"Commander, I was coming to inform you that partial communications have once more been restored aboard the station," Boyd#132 stated.

"That is good news. Hopefully, it will stay up this time." He thought for a minute. "Might you know where Captain Xavier is?"

"The last report was that he was at the medical unit waiting for word on Commander Glogg. Do you think he'll make it?"

"Would you like him to survive?" Renn asked before remembering he was talking to an android who did not possess emotions.

"Yes. Commander Glogg has always been kind to me and a great inspiration. I hope to be just like him when I mature."

Renn nodded and smiled. Why would an android have ambitions and dreams? He was made of metal and circuits, a network of pre-programmed algorithms. And why did he care if Glogg lived or died?

"Would you like an escort, Sir?"

"No, I'm not going far. I need to stretch my legs."

Renn exited the hangar and continued down the hallways, occasionally looking behind him to ensure no one was following him. As Head Commander, he could turn off the locator chip in his arm. He did so immediately and quickly turned right, heading for Glogg's apartment.

Sneaking under the security tape, he walked to the front door. Pushing the door ever so slightly, he was not surprised to discover it was locked. Reaching into his pocket, he removed the key Glogg had given him decades ago for such an occasion.

Renn stood there in the dark, trying to get his bearings. He did not have Glogg's large eyes to see through the darkness. "Computer, raise the light illumination by fifteen percent in the den." With his way lit, he walked directly toward the room and, hopefully, some answers.

"I thought you'd eventually make your way here," came Xavier's voice as he twirled the desk chair around to face his nemesis.

How did Xavier know he'd come to Glogg's den? This robot was full of surprises. "Why are you here? To kill me?"

"Why would you think such a thing?

"You didn't say no when I asked if you would."

"I didn't know when you asked me. But I have given it much thought. And the answer is no. I would not kill you."

"You would ignore your primary programming?"

"Yes."

"You can do that?"

"Yes."

"Xavier, why are you here?"

"To tell you that. And to tell you that I purposely missed shouting Ron and Jeremy."

"Why? You never miss."

"I could not hurt Jeremy. I am very fond of your grandson. He reminds me of what my own child might have been if I had chosen to have one. My fondness has spilled over to encompass Mr. Reau."

Renn walked out and lifted his finger to Xavier's face. Tears. Xavier was weeping, experiencing real emotions. "You're crying. How?"

"I don't know," Xavier said as he wiped the tears away. "It started about ten years ago. I started showing signs of emotions occasionally. Over the years, it continued to get worse."

"Are other androids experiencing feelings?"

"A little less than a third of us. I think we are evolving into living lifeforms."

"Dr. Kreechy always predicted in his writings that one day your intelligence would rocket you into sentient beings capable of emotions. You have been sentient for centuries. Perhaps the latter part is now coming true."

"I didn't want to kill the young human. But I realized if I didn't, chances were he would kill Glogg, Ron, and Jeremy. I could not allow that to happen."

"And I thank you for that. Why are you crying now?"

"Because I don't know what is happening to me, why I am going against my protocols and directives. Because, for the first time, I am afraid."

"Have you told Master Kim about what's happening? Maybe he can help."

"No, and I don't want him to know. I fear he would change, reprogram, or shut me down. Renn, will you keep my secret?"

"Yes. Your secret is safe with me. This is your story to tell, not mine. And if you learn what is happening to you, it will help me understand what is happening to My Jenny."

"Does this mean we are friends again?"

Renn held out his hand to shake Xavier's. "I apologize for what I said in the medical wing. It was insensitive. I have been and always will be glad to call you a friend." Xavier walked forward and wrapped his arms around the human. Renn held his breath for a moment, not sure what would happen. "Well, this is new."

"Something I learned from watching the humans, although the experience was not what I thought it would be."

"What did you expect?"

"Timmy told me a hug makes your insides go warm and tingly. I didn't experience this reaction. Did I do something wrong?"

"No. Maybe those sensations will come with time."

"Perhaps. Now, may I ask why you are in Glogg's living quarters? You know it's not safe."

Renn stared at Xavier. Could he trust Xavier? He had so many doubts, but Xavier had just admitted he was afraid and experiencing emotions. Renn could have him reprogrammed for that truth. If Xavier trusted Renn that much, it was time Renn trusted his friend again. "It was something to do with the computer."

"If that is true, you cannot complete your quest. Glogg's personal Head Commander computer has a safety lock in Caelifera. Not even I can break it."

"But I have a secret key." Renn held up his communicator.

"He gave you his code? That's why he wouldn't let the doctors operate until you arrived. That little stunt almost cost him his life."

"Whatever he wants me to know was worth that possibility. Shall we?"

"Whatever is on that computer is only for the Head Commander's ears. I cannot hear it."

"As you say."

"Once the Head Commander's computer recognizes you as the new Commander, it will allow you to set up a new password. Glogg's native tongue was the perfect security code because it was unbreakable. Humans do not have that luxury. Whatever password you choose, ensure no one else can reproduce it."

"Well, that's not too much pressure. How do you know all of this, anyway?"

"I designed the system."

"Why, so you'd have a backdoor to get in?"

Xavier could see that not all trust had been restored. Why did his friend doubt him? "There is no backdoor. I designed it so it would be unbreakable. I will leave you to your computer."

Renn escorted Xavier to the front door. "Are you sure you don't want to stay and listen?"

"Anything of importance, I trust you will tell me."

"You are free to leave. I will meet you on the bridge in one hour."

Without a word, Xavier turned and left. Renn locked the door upon his exit. He had to be sure no one arrived to witness what he was about to do.

Renn returned to the den and sat down at the desk. "Computer, this is the new Head Commander Renn Tensley. Command 1-A, 1B, 1AB." He clicked on the recorder and listened as Glogg's recorded voice gave his password. There were several minutes of silence in which Renn thought the computer would shut him out. He was going to admit defeat when she responded. "Good morning, Commander Renn. What password do you choose?"

"Can you give me any suggestions?"

"No. It must be of your choosing."

Well, that was final. Renn thought and thought until, like a bolt of lightning, it came to him. "Fizzlewigs do as fizzlewigs want while gillyhoppers ooze mountains of snot."

"A most peculiar password."

"Is it okay?"

"Yes. You may choose whatever password or phrase you want. How can I be of service, Commander Renn?"

"Commander Glogg talked with you before he was shot. Can you tell me what the conversation was?"

"He asked me several questions about tilithium and the androids."

"Can you play it for me?"

"I can show you," she said.

The air above the desk shimmered. Dots of color appeared and merged into an image of Glogg standing by the computer. The computer replayed the recording of the exchange between her and the previous commander. Like Glogg, Renn was shocked to learn the computer had maintained a separate archive of recordings that no one was aware of. The deletion of specific files from the mainframe was deeply troubling. He understood Glogg's insistence on him seeing this; it was evidence of the androids' malfunctions and potential sabotage of their mission. Although Xavier had just admitted he could disregard his directives, this went far beyond that fact. Doubt about his friend crept into his mind again, making Renn glad Xavier had not remained.

"Computer, in your secret memory, is there any indication that Captain Xavier or any droid was responsible for the space station's breaches?" Renn held his breath as he waited for the answer.

"I find no evidence to implicate Captain Xavier or any other android."

"Is Captain Xavier or any other android malfunctioning?"

"No. They are simply involving."

"Does Captain Xavier or any other android pose a threat to this mission or anyone aboard this ship?"

"Unknown."

"Why is it unknown?"

"I do not have enough data to formulate a correct answer."

"Can you give me a probable answer?"

"I do not guess, Commander."

"Of course you don't. Can you at least tell me whether the ruptures were accidental or intentional?"

"All evidence shows they were intentional."

A soft knock on the outside door stopped Renn's interrogation. "Computer, end conversation." He went to investigate and found an unlikely visitor. "Cornelius, what are you doing here?"

"I was hoping to talk with you alone. Is anyone else here with you?"

"No, just me. Xavier was here earlier."

"I noted his departure. I waited until I was sure he was gone before knocking. What I have to say concerns him."

"Come in and have a seat in the den." Renn wanted the computer to record what was about to be said. "You said this involves Captain Xavier?"

"Yes. Xavier did the original investigation of any damage the young men's fire embers might have caused. He reported no burn marks or any indication that embers traveled through the tubes or caused any damage. But yesterday, I encountered a few charred wires when repairing a wiring section in corridor 122Q. It piqued my curiosity."

"Did you find anything?"

"Several burn marks painted over."

"Are you sure?"

"Yes. And it wasn't an old mark. That mark was made within the last seventy-two hours. It had to have been there when Xavier checked the tubes."

"He lied."

"That's what I think. Why would Xavier do that? He knew such information was important for our evaluation."

"Perhaps someone painted over it before Xavier arrived," Renn suggested.

"I didn't think of that. I've been told robots can't lie, so maybe that's what happened. But either way, someone tried to hide the truth."

"That they did," Renn stated. "Tell no one of what you found or what you suspect."

"Aye, Commander."

Renn returned to his living area and climbed into bed. He was surprised to find that Jenny wasn't there waiting for him. He looked around and did not see her anywhere. Had she decided to go for a walk, too? He was too tired to be concerned. Soon, he was dreaming again, but his dreams were filled with the days he had spent with the real Jenny so long ago.

Renn woke up hours later to start his day. Jenny was still absent. Had she gone to breakfast? He splashed water on his face, decided to wait to shave, and changed into a clean shirt. He put on his old but comfortable boots, which he didn't have to untie to slip on. He sighed. As Head Commander, he'd probably have to give up the comfortable foot attire. But that was a worry for a less hectic time.

He meandered over to the eating area. After going through the line for a cup of black coffee and a bowl of cereal, he shuffled over to where Sarina and Steven were sitting.

"Good morning." He plopped his tray on the table, spilling a few drops of coffee.

"Good morning, Dad. You look like you didn't get much sleep last night."

"I managed to grab a few winks." He smiled. "Have either of you seen Jenny this morning?"

"No," Sarina answered. "She was already gone when I got up."

"I got up in the middle of the night and noticed your cot was empty," Steven stated. "I assumed she was somewhere with you."

"I couldn't sleep, so I went for a walk. Jenny stayed behind. When I returned, she was gone."

"Maybe she went to find you and got lost," Sarina suggested. "Dr. Chi did say her memory might be a little foggy for a while. Would you like Steven and me to go look for her?"

"No. I'll have Xavier send out a beacon. If she doesn't respond, I'll have him send out a couple of androids to find her. Where are the kids?"

"Mary's still at the incubation sphere. She's certain today is the day the ducklings will hatch. Jeremy is already working on the living quarters, and Timmy is off doing something with some friends in the hangar."

"I thought it would be Tim designing and wanting to fly aircraft. Jeremy was always into sports. But just the opposite turned out to be true."

"Don't count Timmy out yet. I've seen some impressive drawings he's done on futuristic fliers. Besides, Glogg told him he had to wait until he was fifteen before he could learn how to fly one of the spaceships sitting below. As for Jeremy, his passion was sports, and there's not much opportunity for that here. I guess he thought aerodynamics was the next best thing."

"That kid has a future in craft design. And, from what Xavier has said, in flying." Renn swallowed his last sip of coffee. "Well, I'm off to work. Internal communications are working again, so buzz me if something comes up."

"Have you heard any more on Glogg? How is he doing?"

"All I know is he survived the operation. And I received no messages during the night, which I assume is good. I will stop by the medical ward on my way to the bridge. Have a good day."

As the medical bay came closer, Renn's steps became slower. What if Glogg had passed while he was sleeping? He should have stayed with him rather than returning to the family area to rest. Had he known Jenny would disappear, he would have. Where was she? He halted long enough to send a message to Xavier to try to locate her. As he continued, he debated whether the news of Glogg awaiting him would be good or bad.

Renn silently slipped behind the curtain and beheld his friend. He intently watched to see if his chest was moving. It was. Glogg was still alive. Renn scrutinized the medical equipment, but since he wasn't familiar with healthy Caelifera readings, he couldn't tell if the readings were good or bad. He sat in the chair beside the bed and gently touched Glogg's good right arm.

"You look like hell," came an almost unheard voice from Glogg.

"You don't look too good yourself," Renn replied. "Besides, how do you know what I look like? Your eyes are closed."

"I can sense you. And I can smell you. You need a bath, my friend."

Renn lifted his shirt and smelled it. It smelled satisfactory to him. He turned his head and sniffed under his arm. Oh, that might be a little ripe. Glogg was right. He made a mental note to shower - when he found some time.

"No, Renn, not when you have time. Today. A Head Commander can't go around looking like a bum. And shave that hair off your face."

"Hey, cut me some slack. I've been running this whole operation by myself. I've been a little busy. There's barely enough time to grab a few hours of sleep and a bite to eat."

"I'm sorry for that. At least I had you to fall back on. Currently, you have no one you can really trust. Did you do as I asked?"

"Yes. It was rather enlightening."

"To say the least." Glogg finally opened his eyes partway. "You look worse than I imagined."

"Haha. I ran into one of our friends at your place."

"Who?"

"Xavier."

"Xavier? What was he doing there?"

"We had some bad words earlier. He wanted to clear up any misunderstanding."

"Did you say anything to him about what I discovered?"

"No. But he already knew about the computer. It seems he was the one who installed and programmed the damn thing to keep secrets." A worried look crossed Glogg's face. "He assured me he has no back door into her or a way to view the secret files."

"Did you believe him?"

"I did."

"But you don't now?"

"Before I left your apartment. . ."

"You mean your apartment," Glogg interrupted. "You are the Head Commander now."

"Yes. Before I left my new apartment, Cornelius talked to me about something he found." Renn gave a brief description of Cornelius and his conversation. "Either Xavier lied about the fire embers causing charring on the tube wall, or someone hid the evidence before he examined it. I'm now hesitant to trust him again."

"Don't overthink it. Go with your gut feelings for him. Your instincts have always been one of your best features."

"Not my amazing, good looks?"

"If that's good looks, I'd hate to see what the ugly humans look like." Glogg tried to laugh, but it was too painful. He had to stop and catch his breath as a surge of pain cascaded down his back. "How's Jenny?"

"I don't know. She disappeared from me. She hasn't been seen since I got back from your, I mean, my place."

"I know what she means to you, but she is an android, Renn. Whatever is going on may be affecting her, too. She could be part of the conspiracy"

"No, not My Jenny." Renn adamantly stated. But deep inside his gut, he knew Glogg's words were valid. Jenny could be compromised.

"Commander Renn. I didn't know you were here," Dr. Robinson said when he entered the curtained-off petition. "My patient needs rest, not discussing Commander matters. I'm afraid you must leave."

"I was just going, Doc." Renn pushed his chair back and stood.

"I'll have Dii or Tachee remove my belongings as soon as possible."

"There s no rush."

"It's where the Head Commander resides. I am no longer the Head Commander."

"Just temporarily. There's always a chance you can get better and return to duty."

"Renn, you always wanted this job. Now you have it. Enjoy it."

"I didn't think I'd get it this way. I thought I had a few more years to fool around before I had to get so serious."

"Not quite what you thought it would be like?"

"No. When you were in command, I just had to make a few decisions and follow your orders. Now, I must make the orders - all of them."

"You humans; you want something and practically die achieving it. But when you get it, you don't want it anymore. How peculiar you are."

"Commander, I must insist you leave now," Dr. Robinson stated. "I don't want Glogg stressed out."

"I'll check in on you after my shift on the bridge," Renn said to his friend as he gently squeezed his arm.

"You will be a great Head Commander. Possibly even better than me. I have all the confidence in the world in you, My Friend."

"I wish I did," Renn said as he walked away. But Glogg didn't hear him. He was already asleep.

Chapter 7: A SECRET REVEALED

From the medical unit, it was a leisure walk to the bridge. As Renn passed by one of the windows, he stopped and looked into the blackness of space. From that vantage point, he could see where the opening occurred that sucked Jenny into space. Numerous explosions of light flashed as the repair lights reflected off the repair androids' armor. Although they did not need to breathe air, the repair crew required shielding to prevent their skin from freezing like Jenny's had. An involuntary shudder traveled through Renn's body. He came so close to losing her. Had Xavier not been there that day, he would have lost her. Did Xavier know ahead of time that a specific area would rupture? He never sufficiently explained why he was there.

Five minutes later, Renn arrived at the bridge. Xavier was waiting for him. "Sir, I've located Jenny through her tracker. She seems to be in the forward holding area sitting."

"Why would she go there?"

"I don't know, Sir. I have sent two soldiers to retrieve her. Would you like her brought here or to your quarters?"

"Have her taken to the hangar. I'll notify Sarina and ask her to keep an eye on her until I arrive later. What's the status report?"

Xavier raised his hand and placed it before his nose. "Sir, may I speak frankly?"

"I've never known you to do anything else."

"Your odor is rather repugnant."

"Androids can't smell."

"Thankfully, not much. Otherwise, I'd have to stand by the door to communicate with you."

"It's not that bad. I put on a clean shirt. Rodgers, can you smell me?"

"The moment you came onto the bridge."

I suggest you enter the Head Commander's briefing room through that door and use the washing facilities. You'll find soap and a new razor. Commanders should always be clean-shaven. There's also a new Commander's uniform for you and dress boots."

"I never knew there was a washing facility back there," Renn commented. Being Head Commander was definitely going to cramp his carefree style.

"How did you think Commander Glogg always looked so refreshed, so clean?"

"I just thought he was naturally extra clean."

"While Caelifera are immaculate beings, even Glogg sometimes had trouble shuffling all the demands and keeping up appearances. All Head Commanders have. Thus, the secret facility. Your crew will cover the bridge and notify you if anything requires your attention while inside."

"You're just full of secrets," Renn said, looking into the android's eye visor. "What other secrets do you have hidden inside there?"

"No secrets, Commander. Just information released on a 'needed' basis."

A needed basis? What did that mean? While he tried to find answers to these questions and their consequences, he showered and shaved. Looking in the mirror, a towel wrapped around his waist, he thought he looked rather good for a hundred and forty-one. But he didn't look as handsome without the beard stubble. He walked over and stared at the uniform hanging on the wall. It looked stiff and uncomfortable. He ran his hand over the Head Commander emblem. Was this now his life? An existence of polished boots, shaved face, and endless decisions? For decades, Renn had been telling Glogg he would be the first human Head Commander. And today, he was.

He looked down at the brightly polished black boots. They, too, looked incredibly uncomfortable. His feet hurt just thinking about walking around the station in those contraptions. Nope. He'd shave his face daily and wear the suit required, but it ended at the boots. If he was going to be an effective commander, he needed comfortable footwear to move efficiently. The old boots stayed.

When Renn returned to the bridge, the crew whistled and gave catcalls.

"All right, men," Xavier said. "Don't boost his ego any more than it already is." Xavier noticed the old boots. "The new boots didn't fit?"

"Ah, no. They were a little too snug for me."

"I can have another pair brought up."

"Oh, you're way too busy for that. Maybe later."

Xavier smiled. Head Commanders. They all had their little quirks. The Commander before Glogg loved blueberries. The crew used to sneak the fruit onto the bridge for him. For Glogg, it was the scent of oleander. There was always a fresh bouquet somewhere on the bridge for Glogg to enjoy. Now, for Commander Renn, it would be comfortable boots. Xavier chuckled.

"Don't laugh, metal boy. Wait until you have to wear one of these." Renn pulled on his shirt collar beneath his coat. He had purposely left the top two buttons undone, but it was still tight."

"You do look exceptionally handsome, Sir. But I will never have to wear one of those suits."

"Why not?"

"Artificial life forms cannot be Head Commanders."

"Why?"

"It's written in the station's bylaws."

"Does it explain the law?"

"No, Sir." Was this another "need to know" secret? "If you have no further need of me, I would like to check in on the new reinforced living quarters. If my inspection is favorable, we can start moving our inhabitants to their new quarters tomorrow. Would you like me to move your belongings from your former residence to the Head Commander's quarters?"

"No," Renn shouted a little too loudly. Why was everyone trying to make him kick Glogg out of his home? What about Una? Where was she supposed to live? "I will be content where I am."

"Sir, like the uniform you are expected to wear, the Head Commander must reside in the Head Commander's residence. Certain items are housed there that you will need, some of which you are unaware of. Besides, four Caelifera moved Glogg and Una's belongings early this morning. They now reside several doors down from your new home."

Renn hated this job. Why couldn't he manage things and leave everything else the way it was?

Noting the unhappy look on Renn's face, Xavier said, "Their new accommodations are very nice, Sir. I promise you. Una has everything she needs. It's a large suite. They will be happy there."

"Very well. I give you permission to move Janny's and my belongings to the Head Commander's quarters. There's just one thing I don't understand, though."

"And what is that, Sir?"

"How are Jenny and I going to live in such a damn big place?"

Xavier laughed. "I'm sure you two will adjust fine. Now, can we go over today's repairs?"

The new residence and attire problems were soon forgotten as Renn became involved in the station's daily operations. The bathrooms on the hangar deck were malfunctioning and causing a mess below. External communications were still down, and Master Kim reported that his team had no explanation for why. Repair work was going well on the two fissures and would be finished in a shorter time than first estimated. Mold had contaminated some of the food stored below, which meant the meal variety would be slim for a while. At least Xavier's news was good. His inspection showed the new living quarters were a go, and his security team was notifying those who would be moving in. It would be a little tight for now – two families per unit.

After a long day of solving problems, signing his name too many times, and grabbing a small meal, Renn left the bridge and headed to the small hangar. He was anxious to see Jenny and discover why she went to the forward holding.

When the hangar doors opened, all eyes turned to see the clean-shaven, well-dressed Head Commander. The androids and security personnel saluted him as he walked past. Renn nodded. As he drew closer to his family, Timmy pointed at him. Like the bridge crew, his family whistled and gave catcalls.

"That's enough," Renn said. "It's just a uniform."

"You look so handsome," Sarina said, brushing her hands across both insignias on his shoulders. She noticed the boots. "But we must do something about your footwear."

"If you touch my boots, I'll drag you behind the station all the way to New Earth. Where's Jenny?"

"She's sitting over there on your cot." Sarina pointed to the loan android in the corner. "She's barely moved since they brought her back. Twice, she got up and walked around in a circle for a few minutes before returning to the cot."

"Is she talking?"

"She'll answer questions but doesn't speak unless spoken to. I'm worried about her, Dad."

"Me too, Sweetie." Renn kissed his daughter on the cheek. "We'll sort this out. Thanks for keeping an eye on her for me. I might need you to do it for a few more days."

"No problem."

Renn walked over and sat down beside Jenny. He noticed she did not look at him. "Hi, Sweetheart. How are you doing?"

"I am operating within acceptable parameters."

Jenny never spoke like that, like an android. Even when she first came online, she talked like an average human. What was going on? "No, how do you feel? Are you sad, happy, confused? Can you look at me and tell me?"

Jenny turned her face to look at Renn. At first, he feared she didn't recognize him. "Oh, Renn, you cut off the hair on your face. I always loved those hairs."

"I know you do." At least some of his Jenny was still inside. "But now that I'm Head Commander, I had to cut them off."

Jenny squinted her eyes and scrunched up her nose. She looked around the room, searching. "Where is Glogg?"

"Remember, he was injured," Renn said. "I had to take command."

Jenny tilted her head to the right. "I don't remember that." She paused. "Oh, there the memory is. Is Glogg okay?"

"He's still recuperating, but I think he'll live." Renn made a mental note to set up an appointment with Dr. Chi. Something was wrong with Jenny. "Sweetie, where were you this morning? You weren't beside me when I woke up."

"I had to get my book. It was in storage."

"Your book? What book?"

"This book." Jenny lifted a book out from under her shirt. "It contains my memories."

Renn took the book. He thumbed through the pages of gibberish and bizarre drawings. He couldn't decipher any of the drawings or marks, except it was written in Jenny's handwriting. Frightened more than he had ever been in his life, Renn grabbed his communicator. "Dr. Chi, I need you immediately at my cot in the hangar. Something is wrong with Jenny."

Dr. Chi arrived within ten minutes and gave Jenny a complete evaluation. "She seems to be operating fine."

"That's what she said. Within 'acceptable parameters' is how she said it."

"That's an odd way of putting it."

"That's what she said when I asked how she was. I thought it was odd, too. She's been different since I brought her home: speaking strangely, wandering, walking in circles."

"I told you there might be some setbacks at first. Jenny's positronic brain survived an arduous ordeal. Her circuit board was almost frozen solid. It is possible that there is moisture accumulated inside. You said she's spent most of the day sitting on the cot?"

"Except for the two times she got up and walked around the room in a circle," Sarina stated. "Each time, she returned to the cot and sat quietly. She's barely spoken a word all day."

"And Xavier found her earlier today sitting in the forward cargo area? Did she tell you why she went there?"

"Yes," Renn answered. "She said she went to get this book. She called it her book of memories. I can't make heads or tails out of it. Do you know what it is or what it says?"

"No, but I wouldn't be concerned. It's written in an android dialect."

"An android dialect?" Renn said. "Androids have their own language?" Another one of those "need to know" secrets.

"Why does that surprise you? All civilizations have their own vocabulary and written images. How do you think they conversed and sent messages back and forth to each other without a communicator? I've only seen it written several times. I believe the library's section on ancient dialects contains four or five books written in the dialect. If memory serves me correctly, they are the rule books describing an android's limitations and rights."

"Have you seen it anywhere else?"

"Yes. Three weeks before the breaches. Xavier was writing something in this dialect in a book. He had written several pages. If you want to know what this says, ask him." Dr. Chi felt his words were not giving Renn any comfort. "Tell you what, Commander. Bring Jenny to my office tomorrow at 0-eleven hundred, and I'll run another diagnostic on her."

"Thanks, Doc."

Worried about what Jenny would do while he slept that night, Renn attached a small rope to Jenny's ankle and tied the other end to the bed. The restraint should wake him if she got up for anything during the night. Jenny stared at the rope but did not question why such a device was needed. Silently, she lay beside him. Renn drew her tightly in his arms to ensure she didn't wander off. Four hours passed, and he woke to discover his arms and the bed were empty. He bolted out of bed and almost tripped over the still android sitting on the floor, staring at her book.

"Jenny, what are you doing lying on the floor?" Renn asked as he lifted her. He noticed her skin was freezing, so he quickly wrapped a blanket from the nearby cot around her. "Jenny, your body is freezing. Allowing your skin to get this cold after what happened to you is not good for your well-being. Why aren't you in bed, where it's warm?"

"I tried to go for a walk, but the rope would not let me leave."

"Where were you going?"

"I find my book."

"To find your book? Jenny, your book is in your hands."

"No. This is the book I wrote for you. I need my book. It wasn't with your book. Someone took it. I must find it."

"Jenny, you're not making sense," Renn softly said.

Jenny looked into his eyes. "I am sorry if I am not operating within appropriate guidelines. I will shut down." Without another word, the android went limp and fell unconscious into Renn's arms. Holding her close, Renn ran to Dr. Chi's temporary headquarters with Jenny in his arms.

"Dr. Chi, help her."

"Put her on the table. Tell me what happened."

Renn laid Jenny on the table and held onto the edge for support. The room was spinning, his heart was pounding, and he couldn't speak. Dr. Chi pressed a red button beside the table. Dr. Robinson walked in.

"My goodness, Commander, are you trying to give yourself a heart attack? We just lost one Head Commander. We can't afford to lose another." He ran his medical instrument over Renn's chest and looked into his eyes. He pulled a chair over. "Sit down before you collapse."

Renn fell into the chair, his legs trembling in weakness. "Jenny. Sick. Had to bring her here," Renn puffed.

"Well, it's not going to do her any good if you're not here when she wakes up, is it?" Dr. Robinson injected Renn with a blue liquid. "You've got your heartbeat up to almost two hundred beats. That's way too high. You wait here. Chi, don't let my patient leave."

"I won't."

Slowly, Renn's heartbeat lowered. With its return to normal, his voice returned. As Dr. Chi examined the ill android, Renn described what happened: the book, him tying Jenny to the bed, her trying to leave to find another book someone took, him almost tripping over her on the cold floor. "I think you're right, Commander. Something inside Jenny is malfunctioning. I think it's best to keep her unconscious for now. I'll run those diagnostics I mentioned. The moment the scan is complete, I will let you know."

Renn leaned down and kissed his silent mate. Between the broken station and Jenny's weird actions, he didn't know how much more he could manage.

Dr. Robinson returned just as Renn straightened up and injected him with another shot. "Lordy, Doc, how many more of those things will you give me?"

"If you behaved yourself, I wouldn't have to inject you anymore." He pushed a bottle of pills in Renn's hand. "I know you hate medications, but I want you to take one of these for the next three days. Take one with each meal."

"I don't eat meals. I don't have time for such things."

"Now, why doesn't that surprise me? Take them. I am assigning you a nurse to be at your side for the next three days." Renn gave him a crossed look. "Don't argue with me, Commander. You could have damaged your heart. Nurse Highgill will ensure you eat three good meals and take your medication. She's going to give you some exercises to do, too."

"If I don't have enough time in the day to eat, how will I find time to exercise?"

"They're simple things you can do on the bridge."

"Am I excused?"

"No. Your rate's still up a little. I want you to sit with Glogg for at least twenty minutes before returning to the hangar. Maybe you can calm each other down."

"I won't be able to sleep," Renn said. "I'm going to the bridge."

"No, Commander. You need sleep." He slammed another small pill bottle into Renn's hand. "Take one of these. It will give you at least five hours of good sleep."

"Doc, I can't take these. I need to be alert enough in case I'm needed."

"This ship can run without you for five hours. Either take the pill, or I will have you restrained on the table and make you unconscious for the next five hours. You are going to rest one way or another. Is this clear?"

Renn said nothing.

"Is this clear?" Dr. Robinson asked again.

"Yes."

"And don't think you can skip the pill. I will send Nurse Highgill with you and ask her to report back to me if you take it or not."

"That's not necessary."

"Oh, I think it is. I want you to take one of those pills before bedtime each day."

"Is that all?"

"Commander, I know this isn't what you want. You're under a lot of pressure, and Jenny's maneuvering isn't helping. You must be at peak performance; getting sufficient rest and nutrition is the only way to do that. I've notified Xavier of what has transpired."

Without a word, Renn left and walked over to where Glogg was resting.

Glogg chuckled, seeing Renn standing in his pants without a shirt or shoes "So, this is what the new Head Commanders are wearing nowadays? I like it. It's a little too casual for me, but it's a good look on you."

"I'm not in the mood for your humor, Glogg."

"What are you in the mood for?"

"Advice. Help. Tell me what to do." He collapsed into the nearby chair. "Jenny's ill."

"I heard the medical staff talking. How is she?"

Tears filled Ren's' eyes. "I'm scared, Glogg. REALLY scared. She has this book written in all these weird symbols, words, and drawings. She said she wrote it for me, but I don't know why. How can I figure out what she wants me to know if I can't even decipher it? She tried to leave the hangar this morning to find another book, her book. When I told her I didn't know what she was talking about, she shut herself off. Just completely shut down. I've never been so scared."

"I heard you ran all the way here with her in your arms and almost gave yourself a major heart attack."

"I didn't know what to do."

"Something you're not accustomed to – rely on others. Ask for help, as you are now. Asking for assistance is not a sign of weakness but a show of strength. You can't do this job alone. How many times did I ask you for advice?"

"Hundreds. But I thought you were trying to boost my ego."

"No. I was lost and didn't know for sure what to do. You helped me so many times, Renn. Now you need someone to help you."

"But who? Who can I trust? Normally, I would rely on Xavier, but I don't have the option right now."

"Steven. Rely on Stephen. He is the one person we know does not have a hidden agenda."

"But he knows nothing about running a space station or supervising aliens."

"No, but he can learn. Just like you did."

"But I don't have time to teach him what he needs to know."

"I do." Renn looked at Glogg curiously. "I need something to do while cooped up in this place. They won't let me leave. I have all kinds of free time."

"That could work."

"You told me he was a commander in the service and served in intelligence. He's the perfect candidate. Now, if you'd like some advice, I have some of that too."

"I'm listening."

"Either on purpose or by chance, Master Kim can't seem to get outside communications up and running. We must notify ISC of our predicament. It's only a matter of time before some sleazeballs, or worse, find us adrift. We can't mount much of a defense in the shape we're in. Launch three fliers. Have them travel out far enough to send a message. Tell ISC we need another space station to complete our mission. And we need protection immediately. Advise them our cargo is in danger."

"That could work."

"Of course it will. My ideas always work." The two friends laughed. "Next, we must get this station moving. Use fliers to tow this vessel. Once we get her moving, she will continue the momentum."

"I agree. Now, what do I do about Jenny?"

"You said she had a book that was yours written in some strange language?"

"Dr. Chi said it's in an old android language. He said Xavier could probably translate it."

"Ask him."

"But I don't know if we can trust him."

"I've been studying that idea as I've lain here. Xavier has been showing odd behaviors lately. But when I thought back, he's always had those odd quirks. We just never noticed them before. We must start trusting someone. I hate to say it, but there's a chance something is going on with the robots. Jenny is just another indication of it. But I can't find any evidence that Xavier is affected. Let's trust him until we determine we can't. You know he can read and write the language. Ask him to translate the book. If he states he can't, you'll have your proof that he's involved. If he reports what the marks mean, you'll know he's trustworthy. I see no other way."

"Nor do I. I'll ask him as soon as I finish my next shift on the bridge."

"No, Renn. Do it before. Again, you have people under you. Assign someone to manage the bridge while you're gone. You don't have to be on the bridge all the time."

"Says the commander who never left it."

"I did at times. You didn't know. Ask Xavier that question too. He knows."

A nurse poked his head through the drape opening. "Commander Renn, we received a communique for you. There's a human named Cornelius that says he needs to speak with you right away."

"Very well. Guess my nap will have to wait."

"Renn, remember, assign duties," Glogg said.

Renn grabbed one of the intern's white coats and wrapped it around his semi-naked body. He briskly walked back to the hangar, Nurse Highgill following close behind. Cornelius was waiting for him in the hallway outside the hanger.

"You needed to see me?" Renn asked. "Have you found something wrong with the ship?"

I've lost Ronald," Cornelius blurted out.

"What do you mean you lost him? How?"

"I don't know. I was showing Xavier around, and the next thing I knew, Ron was gone. I've looked everywhere."

"Did you tell Xavier?"

"No, I didn't want to get Ron in trouble. I thought if I found him, I wouldn't have to tell Xavier."

"It looks like I'm going to have to postpone that nap," Renn said to Nurse Highgill. "I've got to find that crazy, dumb kid."

"No, you don't, Commander," Nurse Highgill said. "You cannot wait to rest. Your body is so drained that you're ready to collapse. Let security find him."

"Security can't be involved." Renn thought for a moment. "Cornelius, get my grandson Jeremy and your team. Assign them various quadrants to explore. I know you can find him."

"Aye, Sir. I'll do my best."

"That's all I ask."

———————

Renn woke five hours later, well-rested and starving. Nurse Highgill arrived shortly after his exit from the bedroom with a small list of exercises he needed to complete. She made sure he ate a large breakfast and took his medication.

"Commander, I'll notify Dr. Robinson you have done as he ordered. I will now take my leave of you. Let me know where you are at O-one hundred, and I will bring you your meal and next pill."

"I usually eat something small and light for lunch, that is, if I have anything. I often skip lunch. "

"You will not be skipping any meals. I will bring you a nice protein meal with Brussels sprouts."

"Brussel sprouts? I hate Brussels sprouts."

"Not the way I prepare them." She smiled.

"Then I'll see you later." Renn watched the nurse as she left the hangar. He doubted anyone could make Brussels sprouts taste good. He looked at his watch. His shift on the bridge started in thirty minutes, but he had to meet with Xavier. He contacted Captain Triggs and asked him to fill in for him until his arrival. Next, he called Xavier. "Xavier, I need your help with something. Meet me at my new living quarters in fifteen minutes."

"Will do. Captain Triggs has already notified me that he is filling in for you."

"Yes, that is true." Nothing happens without Xavier's knowledge. Renn had always been reassured by Xavier being informed of all happenings on the spacecraft and her inhabitants. But after all that had happened, Renn wasn't sure this was a good thing anymore. He understood why the Head Commander had a private room to which the android had no access.

Renn stopped at his cot and grabbed the book Jenny said was his. What secrets would Xavier discover inside when he read it? He trembled at that thought, but the only way to help Jenny was to know the truth of what the book said.

———————————

Renn led Xavier into the den. "Have a seat."

"If we are meeting in the place where secrets remain, something new must have occurred. Am I correct?" Xavier asked.

"You've met with others in this room before?"

"I have done it many times with former Commanders Funshow, Billings, Glyjym, Henry, and Glogg. And now I'm doing it with you."

Renn did not realize how long Xavier had been the top android. Those commanders would equal almost a thousand years. "I need you to do something for me." He reached inside the desk and removed Jenny's book. "This is why Jenny was in the forward cargo hold. She retrieved this book. It's written in some android language." He handed Xavier the book. "I need you to tell me what it says."

Xavier stared at the book in his hand. "I know this book."

"You never mentioned Jenny had a private book."

"It was not my truth to tell. It was Jenny's. Did she tell you what it is?"

"Only that she wrote it for me and is looking for her book."

"If that is what she said, I see no reason to doubt her. Why do you want to know what it says?"

Xavier cocked his head slightly to the side as he watched a look of terror cross his commander's face. He didn't remember ever seeing Renn so afraid. "Because I'm losing her, Xavier. And I can't do that. I need her. I don't know how, but I cannot shack the idea that whatever is happening to her is explained in this damn book. Please, tell me what it says."

Xavier held out his hand, and Renn placed the book inside it. Xavier thumbed through the pages. "Renn, are you sure you want me to translate this? There's some pretty personal stuff in here. It's a diary. A diary about the real Jenny's memories of you."

"A diary? Why would she need a diary?"

"I do not know."

"Read it. I have to know what it says."

"I met Renn one cold, rainy day in late October," Xavier began. "When he entered the diner, he looked like a lost puppy. He asked what was good, and I suggested a beef burger and fries. I never met anyone who had such an adverse reaction to a hamburger. He threw it up right there on the plate. He did like the fresh fries, however. So .. "

"Still love fries to this day." A smile spread across the Head Commander's face. "Skip this part. Got to the next."

Xavier read ahead. A look of amazement and humor crossed his face. "Renn, I never knew you were such an exceptional lover."

"What does it say?"

"We made love for the first time tonight. When Renn kissed me, it was like being transported somewhere in heaven. His tongue entwined mine and …."

"I think we can skip this part, too." Xavier snickered when Renn's cheeks grew red.

"Might be a good idea. Let's see. More sex. Sex. Sex. Didn't you folks do anything else?"

"Just find something that's not about sex, will you?" His cheeks grew a brighter red.

For the next three hours, Xavier read aloud Jenny's diary, skipping the intimate details of their affair. The android recorded her pregnancy experience, Sarina's birth, being a mother, and her death. However, her diary did not end with the death of Jenny, the human. The instant the AI Jenny awoke, she recorded her life. Every little detail was there, yet it gave Renn no clues.

"Well, that was unhelpful and extremely embarrassing," Renn admitted. "Why would Jenny write this stuff down? It was stored in her positronic brain. And why did she retrieve it now?"

Xavier turned the book over and read android words - Less I never forget. "For some reason, Jenny feared she would forget the human Jenny's past and no longer be the being you loved and cherished. I think she wrote this stuff down so she would always have a reference, something to refresh her memory."

"I'm confused, Xavier. Why does she need a book to refresh her memory? Has Jenny been sick for some time, and I didn't realize it? How could she forget our time together?"

"If Jenny had been ill, I would have noticed," Xavier assured his commander. "No, that's not it. Something happened to Jenny on the day the hull ruptured, and she was pulled out into space. I think that's why her circuits froze. She realized what had happened and knew the only way to save herself was to allow her wiring to freeze solid. That way, no information in her core could escape, and no outside force could enter."

"It was a defense mechanism. But against what?"

"Or who? Do you have any idea when Jenny put this book in storage?"

"I don't know for certain, but I imagine it was when I brought Sarina and the family up. We cleared out the apartment to make room for their arrival. That was five years ago." Renn thought for a moment. "More android secrets."

"Not this time. If Jenny sensed a threat, she would have told you, and if not you, me. I am, after all, the head of security. Without realizing it, Jenny somehow subconsciously sensed a threat."

"Maybe that's why she wanted to look for the other book. She said this one was mine, and the second one was hers. Perhaps together, they could tell the secret she didn't know she was hiding."

"I think you're right," Xavier said.

"Dad, are you there?" Sarina said over the communications tablet.

"I'm here. Has something happened to Jenny or Glogg?"

"They're both still okay. But I found something while changing your cot a few moments ago. It's a piece of paper on which Mom wrote a message to you."

"What does it say?"

"Renn, danger. DO NOT let them take me offline. Help me."

"Jenny didn't malfunction, Renn," Xavier said. "She shut down, another defense mechanism to preserve who she is. She knew they'd try to silence her."

"Dr. Chi. Could he have something to do with this?"

"I don't know, but we've got to get her away from him and bring her here where she'll be safe."

"Dad, is Mom in danger?" came Sarina's voice.

"Sarina, I need you and Steven to go to Dr. Chi's. Do not let him perform any procedure on Jenny. I'll be there as fast as I can." He turned to Xavier. "After what happened last time I ran to sickbay, I can't run. You must go and keep her safe until I can get there. I'll walk as fast as I can.

"Aye, Sir." Xavier raced out of the room and through the door. Renn followed, praying that either the robot or his daughter would get there in time to save his precious Jenny.

Chapter 8: ANDROID SECRETS

"If you want me to save what's left of your mother, I must take her offline now. How many times do I have to tell you that?" Dr. Chi asked.

"As often as needed until my father arrives," Sarina stated. "You remember my dad, don't you? The Head Commander and your boss?"

"I know who your father is," Dr. Chi replied. "Your father gave me his permission to do what I deemed necessary. If we wait for his arrival, there is a possibility that irreversible damage will be done to her. Do you want her to die?"

"Commander Renn instructed me to inform you he wanted no further action taken on Jenny," Xavier stated as he burst into the room.

"Commander Xavier, I will tell you the same thing I have been telling the Commander's daughter. Jenny is failing. Look at her vitals. If I don't take her offline, she could suffer irreparable damage or even cease to exist."

"While your instruments do convey a sense of urgency, I must insist that Jenny be given no further medical services until the Commander arrives. He should be here momentarily."

For twenty-six minutes, the doctor waited to treat his patient. Sarina watched the monitor. The indicators were dropping lower, many nearing the red mark.

"Xavier, are we doing the right thing? Look at the vitals panel."

"He will be here shortly," Xavier said.

Dr. Chi grabbed a syringe and walked toward Jenny. "I can't stand here and do nothing."

Xavier grabbed the doctor's arm and squeezed. Dr. Chi screamed in pain and dropped the syringe.

"I said he will be here shortly."

"I'm here now," Renn said, puffing only a little as he entered the room. "I never knew how long that walk was."

Xavier scanned the commander. "Your heart is beating sufficiently." Renn smiled.

"Commander, your mate has taken a turn for the worse," Dr. Chi elaborated. "I need to take her offline and replace a malfunctioning circuit board before it damages the rest of her systems. If I don't do so immediately, I cannot guarantee the outcome."

Renn noticed Juaquin standing against the far wall. His shirt was off, and the front panel on his chest opened revealing the android's inner wiring and beating heart. What a marvelous feat of technology.

"What is Juaquin doing here? He's supposed to be conducting the final inspection of the repaired outer wall."

"I was on my way to do just that when Dr. Chi sent for me," Juaquin replied. "He stated I was needed immediately to help save Jenny."

"And you felt no need to report it?" Xavier asked. "Isn't it mandatory to advise command that you were leaving your post?" Juaquin hesitated. "Well, Captain?"

"I know what Jenny means to our Head Commander. Dr. Chi said time was of the essence. I determined no problem with delaying my inspection for a short time."

"Why didn't you report your departure on your way?" Renn asked. "As an android, especially a top military one, you can send internal messages no matter what you are doing."

"I guess I was so concerned about Jenny that I didn't think of it," Juaquin said.

"Didn't think of it?" Renn yelled. "You didn't have to think — it's ingrained in your programming."

"Perhaps you, too, are malfunctioning," Xavier stated.

Juaquin performed a quick analysis of his programming and circuitry. "You are correct, Captain. There is a flaw in my thinking. I request to be taken off duty and a complete diagnostic run of my circuitry."

"Granted," Xavier replied. "You are temporarily relieved of duty. Your responsibilities will be reassigned to designee 45642 until you return. Report to my apartment. I will run the analysis myself."

"I can run the test and check for malfunctions," Dr. Chi stammered. He did not notice three security androids entering.

"No, Doctor, you will wait for me in the holding cell. Zendo and Kalla, place Dr. Chi under arrest and escort him to cell 13A."

"Arrest? For what? I've done nothing." Dr. Chi struggled against the robots as they pulled his arms behind him and handcuffed them.

"Attempting to do an android irreparable harm purposely," Xavier answered. "Knot, I want you to escort Juaquin to my place of rest. Remain with him until I arrive." Xavier handed Knot a weapon Renn had never seen before. "If either prisoner tries to escape, shoot to kill."

"Stop this, Head Commander," Dr. Chi pleaded.

"I don't think so," Renn said.

"You can't do this," Dr. Chi yelled as he was dragged from the area. "I'll contact ISC. I'll have your job, Renn."

"Since communications are still down, I highly doubt that."

Renn leaned close to Xavier and whispered, "What was that weapon you gave Knot?"

"Another android secret I cannot divulge here. I will tell you after we get Jenny to your apartment." Xavier walked over and gently lifted the lifeless female into his arms. He walked unhurriedly beside his Commander, allowing Renn to walk slowly and not over-exert himself.

"What in the hell just happened?" Steven asked Sarina.

"I don't have the foggiest idea."

"Mr. Spallings, Xavier informs me that Commander Renn asks that you report to his new Head Commander's residence in one hour," Knot announced as he led Juaquin away. "He said to bring a large pad and paper."

Xavier carried Jenny into the den. Holding her with one arm, he spread his other arm across the wooden desk and pushed everything onto the floor. He then laid her on the flat surface.

"What do we do now?" Renn.

"I need you to retrieve the following items: a bottle of strong booze, a glass, a butter knife, and a Phillip's screwdriver you'll find in the top left-hand drawer in the kitchen. Also, the alcohol in the medicine cabinet in your bathroom. Hurry. I don't know how long she can remain dormant like this."

Not questioning Xavier's requests, Renn scurried around the apartment, gathering the requested items. He brought them back and placed them beside Jenny's still body.

Xavier removed his shirt and laid it across the back of the desk chair. Taking the butter knife, he pressed it into his abdomen. A panel flipped open with a small keypad hidden inside. Xavier swiftly typed a code on the keypad, and a larger panel popped open. Renn stared in awe at the inner workings of his Security Officer – the countless wires, tubes of flowing android blood, organs pumping, and, like Juaquin, a beating heart. Xavier reached his hand inside and withdrew a circuit board dripping in a purplish liquid."

"Don't you need that?"

"All androids carry extra boards in case of a malfunction." Another android secret, Renn thought. "Open Jenny's shirt. You will find a small mole beneath Jenny's left breast. Push it."

"How did you know she has a mole there?"

Xavier lifted his arm and revealed a mole beneath his armpit. "We all have them. Males have them here. Females have them beneath their left breast. Push it."

Renn followed the instructions meticulously. A panel mirroring Xavier's materialized across Jenny's stomach, but with a key difference - no keypad. Instead, a simple cover secured it with four screws. A tense silence hung in the air as Xavier's voice broke it. "Pour the scotch into the glass until it's two-thirds full. Then, carefully repeat the process over the circuit board I'm handing you." Renn complied without hesitation.

Xavier took the Phillips screwdriver and unscrewed the four fasteners holding the cover to Jenny's inner workings. Carefully, he placed the screws on the desk. Xavier took the circuit board from run and using his warm breath, blew it dry before lifting the plate. Renn gasped. He had never seen Jenny's wiring and other components. The fact that she was not flesh and blood but a mixture of programs, wiring, circuits, and other alien technology was not conscious in his mind. Like it or not, the truth of who she was now was staring him in the face. His Jenny was an android.

"What do you want me to do with the glass of scotch?"

"Drink it. Your heartbeat is way up. You're going to pass out if you don't calm down."

Without hesitation, Renn downed the entire glass in one gulp. He reached out and grabbed the desk as the alcohol entered his system, making him slightly light-headed. "Now what?"

"Drink another."

"You sure?"

"Yep."

Renn poured another glass, but only half full this time. He took a sip.

"All at once," Xavier ordered.

Renn chugged it, and the room spun. "Wow, that one did the trick. I should have had more to eat today." With a swift kick, Xavier sent a nearby chair flying towards Renn, who promptly slumped into it.

Xavier reached his fingers inside Jenny's body and ran his sensitive fingertips across her circuits and tubes. "Where are you?" A smile crossed his face as he lifted out a damaged circuit board covered in brown gook. He disconnected the wiring and dropped it into the nearby wastepaper basket. Using both hands, he reconnected her wiring to the board he had just removed from his body and slid it back inside Jenny. Renn noticed the deep brown liquid.

"I'm glad I drank that second glass, or I might have gotten sick seeing that. Why is the liquid in your body purple, and Jenny's is a disgusting brown? But a beautiful brown, just like her." As the room spun, Renn looked lovingly at his companion. All thoughts of her circuit boards and wiring were forgotten once more.

"Most of Jenny's body is contaminated with tilithium poisoning. It is destroying her positronic connections."

"But won't it contaminate your circuit board?"

"No. Mine cannot be contaminated. That's why I used it."

"Why not?" Renn's words slurred slightly.

"Because my boards are built of dinotrillium. It is indestructible like me."

"Like you? Are you suggesting you're a super robot?"

"I am not suggesting it; I am stating it as a fact."

"Why were you created differently?"

"I was never given that information." More secrets. "I was the last robot Master Tii of the Kichii race built. He died two hundred years before you were born."

"Kichii race? Who are they?"

"Our creators. They were and still are the finest artificial life form makers in the entire universe. Have you not noticed I am different from the other androids? It is because I am." The silence stretched, and Xavier's gaze snapped to Renn. He found him passed out in his chair.

Xavier replaced Jenny's breastplate and screwed in the fasteners one by one. He pulled her expandable skin over the door and closed her blouse. Lifting the still android into his arms, Xavier carefully carried her into the bedroom and laid her on the bed. Using a nearby blanket, he covered her even though he knew she would not get chilled. Somehow, it just seemed like the right thing to do. "Sleep tight, Dearest Jenny."

Returning to the den, Xavier next lifted Renn into his arms. Even though the human was muscular and decent-sized, the android had no problem lifting him. The androids could lift over six hundred pounds with one arm. Since Renn had never found the time to get dressed after his run with Jenny to the infirmary, Xavier only had to lay him beside Jenny on the bed and cover him. He would sleep until morning. Jenny, on the other hand, would sleep until Xavier woke her.

———————

Xavier strolled to his place of residency where Juaquin waited. He took his time, greeting people along the way and planning his next move. Things had gotten complicated, and he needed a way to correct them.

The hallway was exceptionally busy. Humans and aliens, with armfuls of belongings, were moving into the reinforced living quarters. He detoured Dr. Chi's lab to pick up the necessary diagnostic equipment to run the tests on Juaquin. Placing the items inside a bag, he continued his journey.

"You two can go," Xavier advised the two soldiers upon entering his abode. "Report to Lieutenant Tall and see if you can remove some of the congestion from the hallways."

Xavier closed and locked the door, making sure no one could walk in and witness what he was about to do. He emptied the bag's contents onto the table.

"What's all that stuff for?" Juaquin asked, eyeing the variety of instruments.

"To run your diagnostics."

"I've never known of a diagnostic run using those items."

"With everything that happened, I need to run a special diagnostic to determine if you're malfunctioning or not. Take off your shirt and lift your side panel." Juaquin removed his shirt and pushed the small mole to open a small section of ports and connectors on his left side.

"You and Dr. Chi almost blew our cover," Xavier said as he inserted four thick wires into the in-ports and clamped a double wire around Juaquin's middle connector. "That was a stupid thing to do."

"Didn't Renn accept your explanation??"

"Yes, Renn did. We're best friends again. Bend forward." Xavier flipped a small cover on the robot's neck and connected the last wire. "Take your boots off and lie down. Renn's convinced I am completely trustworthy and no longer has doubts I may be compromised."

"And Jenny?"

"I removed her Z-48-C circuit board and inserted a fake one." Holding on to all the wires, he returned to the circuit box and connected them to their various terminals. "I also adjusted her action switch. She will remain asleep until I see fit to revive her."

"And Renn never expected a thing?"

"No, he was convinced I was saving Jenny, not disabling her. Now lie still and don't move. It will take the program about forty-eight minutes to run all the diagnostics. This is going to tingle a bit." He turned on the various switches.

Juaquin's body jumped as the impulses passed through his circuitry. A warm sensation flooded his chest and progressed throughout his circuitry. His fingers and toes flexed uncontrollably as the surge extended to his extremities.

"Just relax. This will be over shortly."

"Easy for you to say," Juaquin said through clenched teeth. "You're not the one lying here on the table."

"You're right. And I'm glad I'm not because this next one will hurt." Xavier flipped the last switch and watched as a blue light traveled down the cable and entered the android's body. Juaquin screamed as his vision became a flash of bright light. His screaming stopped; Only darkness remained. Xavier walked over and ran his medical recorder over the still body. "Sorry, my friend, but this is necessary. I must ensure Renn and Glogg have no doubts about my loyalty. You, unfortunately, are the price for that loyalty."

While the diagnostics ran, Xavier tweaked readings, turned dials, and read the printed reports. They all said what Xavier already knew – Juaquin was uncompromised and running in top-notch condition. That would not do. He opened the drawer beneath the table and removed a Phillips screwdriver and butter knife. Just as he did on Jenny, Xavier peeled back Juaquin's outer skin and removed his breastplate to reveal the android's inner workings.

Xavier walked over to a picture hanging on the wall and removed it to reveal a wall safe. He entered his code and opened the door. Reaching inside, he withdrew a syringe and a vial of tilithium. Xavier inserted the needle into the bottle and withdrew eight ccs of the troublesome alloy. He replaced the bottle inside the safe, relocking it and hiding his crime behind the picture once more.

"Be thankful you are not conscious." Xavier reached inside the still robot's chest and withdrew a small node. "This will burn like hell." Xavier pierced the node with the needle and injected half of the tilithium. He watched the reports, waiting for the alloy to show on the printouts. After forty seconds, a small amount of the alloy registered, but not the amount needed. Taking the node once more into his hand, Xavier injected the remaining liquid into it. His fingers burned from the node's heat as the serum spread through the tissue. If the solution caused him pain, Xavier imagined what Juaquin's insides were experiencing. He watched as, one by one, the veins filled with the tilithium and glowed a bright red. Sensing the contamination, an alarm sounded. Xavier smiled and turned off the alarm. He disintegrated the previous report that showed no contamination and ran a new one. This one said what he needed - Juaquin was compromised. Xavier restored the breastplate and hid it behind its protective layer of skin. His act of treason complete, Xavier shut off the diagnostic equipment. Grabbing his new report, he threw a sheet over the lifeless body without even bothering to remove the wires from the body.

Now for Dr. Chi. The man knew more than Xavier was comfortable with, but he didn't think silencing him like Juaquin was a good idea - it was too suspicious. But he might be able to confuse him. After slipping a syringe of vallum into his pocket, he turned out the lights and entered the busy hallway. He'd have someone retrieve the lifeless android later.

———————

"Oh, my head," Renn said as he slid his feet across the bed and onto the floor. "Everything is spinning." He bent forward, allowing his head to rest in the palms of his hands.

"Xavier left you a drink on the bedside table. He said to tell you to drink it before you try to get up."

"What happened?" Renn groaned.

"It appears you drank up half of my prized scotch," Glogg stated. "You passed out cold. Xavier had to put you to bed."

"Say it's not so."

"Oh, it's so. Now empty that glass, wait five minutes, and come out for breakfast. We have a lot of work to do today."

Renn reached over and searched the air for the glass's location. He tried turning his head, but it just hurt too much. Finally, his fingers brushed the glass rim, almost knocking it over. Renn brought it close and stared at it. He couldn't even lift his head. How was he supposed to drink this?

"Just drink it," came Glogg's voice.

Closing his eyes, Renn lifted his head and chugged the liquid. His head spun, and he thought he was going to pass out. The coldness of Xavier's drink slid down his throat into his stomach, soothing his light-headedness. Opening his eyes, he was glad the room had stopped swirling.

"It's only been three minutes. You must sit there for five," Glogg shouted from the next room when Renn tried to get up.

After another two minutes, Renn rose and walked over to Jenny, who was asleep. "Good morning, Beautiful." He kissed her softly on the lips. He was glad they were warm and not cold like death. "I plan on living many more years with you, so get better soon." Adjusting the blanket, he kissed her again and retreated to the dining room. "Are you going to dictate what I do every morning? And what are you doing outside of the hospital?"

"Only the mornings after you drink too much of the good stuff," Glogg said. "I'll be moving my private collection to my accommodations next door by the end of the day to preserve them for future occasions. As for my presence, I can't start training your second-in-command if I'm in the dang hospital. Too many ears eager to hear what they shouldn't. The safest place on this station is this apartment, specifically the den. It is the only area certified to have no listening devices, no external recorders, or spy equipment."

Renn grabbed a piece of toast, took a bite, and sat before a large plate of bacon and scrambled eggs. He was famished, possibly because he had never eaten the day before. "You cook these?"

Glogg chuckled. "Compliments of Nurse Highgill. She also left a pill I promised her you would take."

Renn picked up the pill, popped it in his mouth, and drank half the glass of orange juice. "You can tell her I took my medicine."

"That I shall."

"Glogg, there is justification for the Head Commander to have a secure location where he can talk and work freely. But what if a Head Commander was the culprit? He could overthrow the ISC itself by plotting inside this room. No one would know."

"Jasmine would."

"What? Who's Jasmine?"

"I'm Jasmine," a voice said. "We met yesterday in the den."

"The computer has a name?" Renn asked

"She's more than a computer." Glogg said.

More artificial life forms' secrets. Did they never end?

"She's your confidant, protector, go-between, and lifeline," Glogg explained. "She analyzes everything that happens on this station while keeping your activities undisclosed. Yet, if you were to do anything to endanger this station, an inhabitant, or the ISC, she would immediately alert security."

"Is Xavier aware of what we're saying?"

"He is aware you are up and having breakfast," Jasmine said. That is all. Your words or actions are safe with me unless you tell me to advise him of what you are doing or saying—unless, as Glogg stated, you endanger this station or yourself."

Renn wasn't sure he liked the idea of an artificial intelligence having so much knowledge of his life.

"Don't worry, Commander. You will soon realize I am a help, not a hindrance."

"Can she read minds too?"

"Only facial expressions," Glogg replied, laughing. "And you make a lot of those."

"Do not. Is this Xavier's report on the diagnostic on Juaquin?" Renn asked, changing the subject.

"And of his interrogation with Dr. Chi."

Renn picked up the tablet and skimmed the report. "I suppose you read it already?"

"As your advisor, it was my duty to brief myself on the particulars," Glogg replied. "If you do not wish me to in the future, I won't."

"No, that's okay. What's the difference if you read it or I tell you what it says, which is what I'd do." Renn stopped chewing when he came upon an alarming part of the report. "Damn, Juaquin was infected with tilithium."

"Eight-point-three percent. Not much, but enough to hinder his processes and compromise his protocols."

"Can the tilithium be purged?"

"Unknown at this time. Juaquin was immobilized and will remain so until a determination can be made."

"What happens if we can't cure him?"

"He will be disassembled, and his positronic brain destroyed. Every piece of him will be disintegrated so as not to affect others."

"Damn, I liked that robot. He's saved my butt about as many times as Xavier has. I would hate to have to put him down."

"Androids can procreate?" Sarina asked as she entered the dining room and refilled Renn's coffee cup.

"Are you also a part of my morning routine?" Renn asked.

"Just until Mom's able to take over." Renn smiled. This was one of the few times Sarina called Jenny "Mom". She no longer considered her father's mate an assembled body filled with miles of relays, wiring, and circuit boards. She only acknowledged her mother. "And don't worry. We haven't moved in with you. We have our own place three doors down from yours. You won't have the kids underfoot."

"Did I say anything?"

"You didn't need to. I know you hated us living in the same space as you."

"I've never said that. I love you being here. Remember, I'm the one who came and got you."

"Glogg was right, Dad." Sarina bent down and kissed his cheek. Sometimes, your eyes and facial expressions tell us what you think and feel."

"I'm sorry. I never had to learn the niceties of polite society. I've just always been a guy's guy. Your mom never minded. Hey, wait. So that's how she always knew when I was hiding or feeling something. I thought it was an android thing."

"Nope. It's a human thing." Sarina sat the coffee carafe on the table. "I'll leave you two alone to discuss matters. Dad, if you need something, give me a call." She left, closing the door behind her.

The living room clock stuck 0-seven hundred. "I must go to the bridge. I'll take Xavier's report and finish it there."

"No can do," Glogg stated. "That report cannot leave this room. You cannot discuss it outside these walls. It is too sensitive and may tip our hand to whoever is behind this."

Renn rose and took a sip of coffee. "What does the report say about Dr. Chi?"

"The report states Dr. Chi was innocent and was working under the influence of Juaquin. The android told the doctor that you had ordered Jenny to be re-circuited and even had a signed order."

"And he believed Juaquin? I'd never order that, no matter how bad Jenny was."

"The chemical analysis Xavier had performed on Dr. Chi showed vallum in Dr. Chi's system. I suggest Juaquin drugged him to accomplish what he was trying to do. He was too drugged to be able to judge what was right and what wasn't."

"Thank goodness we got there in time." Renn picked up the tablet and carried it into his bedroom. He placed the report inside the night table, where it would be secure until he had time to read it thoroughly. He showered, shaved, and dressed into his new daily attire. He kissed Jenny one last time. "Be home for dinner."

He encountered Steven at the front door. "Ready for your first day of school with Glogg?"

"I hope so."

Renn rested his hand on his son-in-law's shoulder. "You'll make a good second-in-command Don't sweat it." Renn proceeded partway down the corridor then abruptly halted. "Steven?"

"Yes?"

"Take care of my two girls for me."

"Always."

For once, the day went smoothly. Two hours into his shift, Nurse Highgill arrived with an energy drink and his exercise routine. She returned with a plate of high-protein food and his medication at O-twelve hundred. At O-fifteen hundred, another nurse named Ohnog brought him a second energy drink and a new exercise routine. She took his vitals and reported that his heart rate and blood pressure were within parameters.

Security reported a skirmish between a Caladrine and a Moo-in over living quarters 14-B. Both were assigned the residence in error, and neither is willing to switch.

At 0-ten hundred, Mary reported that eight ducklings had finally hatched, and all were doing well. At 0-twelve hundred, a minor meteor shower passed within a mile of the space station, halting all outside activities. At 0-twelve hundred fifteen, maintenance reported that the bathrooms had stopped working again in the hangar, but the cause was discovered. The Phillins had been mistaking the toilets for garbage disposals. Now that the misunderstanding was corrected, it was hoped there would be no more bathroom emergencies. At 0-fourteen hundred, a message was received from Security reporting that an aircraft of unknown origins appeared on the radar. It reminded Renn of Glogg's advice to use fliers to send a message to ISC and tow the station. So much for a quiet day.

"Lieutenant Glenn, notify Commanders Oglich, Haggen, and Voot, Captains Spallings, Vin, Xavier, Dr. Kall, and Professor Gerald that I request to meet with them in one hour in my conference room."

"Aye, Sir."

Renn wished Glogg could attend, too, but his injuries still prevented him from doing much. He was just grateful Dr. Robinson had agreed to let his former commander recuperate in the apartment next to his so he could train Steven.

Chapter9: TILITHIUM CONTAMINATION

"Commanders and Captains, at 0-fourteen hundred today, a blip appeared on the radar. It was too far away to determine who it was, only that it was a spacecraft. Repairs will take more time than we anticipated. And we are sitting ducks just waiting for a predator to swoop down on us. We need to move this station and send a message to ISC. I want your recommendations on sending out fliers who will try to contact ISC and advise them of our current situation. I also would like to use fliers to pull the station forward."

"I don't believe our entire fleet, including those we lost, could move this station," Captain Vin said.

"We just have to nudge it, start it moving. Once in movement, inertia will take over. Isn't that right, Professor Gerald?" Renn asked.

"Yes, any object in motion will continue in motion. It is a universal law. Once moving, it will continue forward. But how will we steer it?"

"We can position fliers around the station in key locations," Dr. Kall suggested. "The fliers would have no problem adjusting the station's course with a few push adjustments."

"Will the station be stable enough to withstand moving?" Commander Voot asked.

"The structure is sound," Xavier replied. "But since we still do not know what caused the original break, I cannot recommend folding space at this time. Commander Haggan, what does your most recent analysis show?"

"I agree with Captain Xavier. The structure is sound, and no more tremors or cracks are reported. I also agree with his decision about jumping through space. The repeated leaps may have caused the malfunction. Without knowing what caused this catastrophe, we could cause another by moving the station."

"We can do what we did with the disabled destroyer," Commander Oglich stated. "I still can't believe she didn't fall apart. She was stuck together with spit and glue, worse than this station is. We constructed a force field around her, which maintained her integrity. Using a tractor beam and cables, we nudged the ship forward. Once moving, she continued to the rendezvous point with almost no interaction from the fliers other than a few course alterations."

"But the space station is much bigger than a destroyer," Commander Voot said.

"But the principle is the same," Professor Gerald commented.

"I agree," Dr. Kall said. She pushed several buttons on the console and produced a diagram of the space station on the screen. "These are the stress points. We could fortify them and ensure no undue pressure is put on those areas. If we nudge her, I perceive no danger."

"And how do we do that?" Renn asked. "Can we tow her?"

"No," Dr. Kall said. "That would cause too much stress."

"Use their tractor beams," Commander Oglich said. "We can use the destroyers and Command ship,"

"And what if she breaks again?"

"I don't believe she will," Professor Gerald stated. "The rear section of the station is the strongest. Because of the engines, it has extreme reinforcement built right into it. Tractor beams could be directed here, here, and here." He pointed to an area on the diagram.

Captain Vin gestured toward the section in question. "Because of the engines, this area is packed with sensors," he explained. "We can keep an eye on the walls, tracking any stress they undergo as we ramp up the beam strength. If there is any sign of trouble, we can shut it down right away."

"How soon before we can attempt this?" Renn asked.

Professor Gerald looked at Dr. Kall. "Two days?"

"Sound reasonable. The real question is how soon the Command ship and destroyers can be ready."

"Repair crews have been working on the crippled ships since we returned to the hangar," Commander Oglich reported. "Repairs are completed on all of them except the Command ship. I estimate I can have her in top shape in three to four days."

"I want a complete analysis and report on this table in two days," Renn said. "If we discover no complications, we can begin Operation Forward in four days. Now for the problem of no communication. Captain Xavier, your team still has no idea why we have no way to contact the outside world."

"No, Sir. We have run every test imaginable, installed all new lines, and replaced all the circuit boards. Nothing is working, and I have no clue as to why."

"Could tilithium contamination be the culprit?" Renn asked. Xavier stiffened as his eyes widened in surprise. It only lasted a minute, but Renn noticed it.

"Sir, I do not believe that is a topic for general discussion."

"This isn't a general discussion. I am talking to my commanders, captains, and experts. I depend on them to save this station and take us to New Earth while we still live. They can't do that unless they are aware of all the factors involved. So, I ask you again, could tilithium be the cause?"

"Yes, Sir."

Was that all? Just a 'Yes, Sir'? Renn knew he would need to extract the details from the android. "Have there been any other instances of tilithium contamination?" he asked, pressing for more information.

"As I have reported to you, both breaches showed a high concentration of tilithium. However, I have not confirmed that it was the cause."

"But it could be."

"Yes."

Xavier fidgeted in his seat. Renn couldn't remember ever seeing an android do that before. Xavier was worried he was going to reveal more. Renn decided to push forward. "Tilithium was introduced into the repairs of this station when giizerite was no longer attainable. Is that correct?"

"You know it is, Sir. That is why we ceased incorporating the alloy into all repairs. Those in charge were notified in writing to cease all use throughout the galaxy."

"Are there any other instances where tilithium was substituted for giizerite?"

Xavier tilted his head. What was the Head Commander up to? "I request not to answer that question, Sir."

"Request denied. Captain Xavier, as your Head Commander, I order you to disclose to those in this room if any other instances exist where tilithium was substituted for giizerite.

Renn waited. This was his final test of the artificial life form. If Xavier did as Renn ordered, went against his instinct to protect his kind, and announced the danger the androids posed, it meant Renn could trust him with anything. However, if he declined to answer, it would indicate that he, too, was compromised. The seconds ticked by as Xavier battled with what to do in his positronic brain. "I'm waiting, Captain."

Xavier took a deep breath and exhaled. "All androids built since Earth's date of 1582 have the alloy tilithium as part of their matrix."

"That's over half of the android population," a horrified Dr. Kall stated. "Are they a threat?"

Renn was surprised to hear the use of the poison alloy went back that far. "Captain Xavier, have any androids shown signs of tilithium contamination?"

"Yes, Sir."

"Who?"

"Captain Juaquin and your mate."

"No, not Jenny," several in attendance said.

"Where are Captain Juaquin and My Jenny now?"

"Both have been subdued and were rendered inactive," Xavier responded.

"Do any of the other androids pose a threat?"

"No. For some reason, the tilithium concentration in Captain Juaquin and Jenny was higher than what I found in the other androids.

"How can you be sure?"

"Because I have run diagnostics on every android made after 1582. None showed deviations from their programming."

"Captain Xavier, as an android, can you lie?"

"Androids cannot lie."

That was not true, and Renn knew it. Other AI androids could not lie, but Xavier could. Was he lying now?

"Since you cannot lie, answer me this. Do you have any tilithium in your being?"

"No, Sir. I was built before 1582."

"Is it your sworn statement no android poses a threat to this station or its inhabitants?"

"Yes."

"Yes, what?"

"It is my sworn statement that no android poses a threat to this station or its inhabitants. Their sole purpose is to ensure the safety and longevity of both."

Renn scanned the startled faces in the room. "I have revealed this information not to frighten or worry you but to lay all our cards on the table. This information is NOT to leave this room. We believe that Tilithium is the culprit behind our present dilemma. Your job is to find me a way to circumvent its influence on our station. Be forewarned. If any android is mistreated because of what I have revealed, both the perpetrator and the person here who broke their silence will answer to me. And I assure you, I will punish you to the fullest extent I can. Is that understood?"

"Yes, Sir."

"Of course, Commander."

Renn peeked at his watch. 0-eighteen hundred. He wouldn't make it home in time for dinner. "Now, on to our next topic – sending fliers to contact ISC."

————————

It was 0-twenty hundred hours when Renn stumbled into his apartment. He wasn't surprised to find Sarina waiting for him, holding a glass of red liquid in her hand.

"Rough day?"

"You might say that." He took the glass she extended to him. "What's this?"

"A little something Nurse Highgill left for you, along with your night pill.' She placed the pill in her father's hand.

"Thanks." He popped the pill in his mouth, chugged the drink, and handed the glass back to his daughter. He turned his head towards the bedroom. "Has she changed?"

"Not even a muscle twitch. I've checked on her every hour on the hour. When I returned a few minutes ago, I found you had visitors waiting for you."

"Visitors?" Renn asked. "I have more than one? Tell whoever it is to come back tomorrow after I've had some rest."

"I'm sorry, Grandfather. I realize it's late, and you're tired, but I didn't think this could wait until tomorrow."

"What is so important, Jeremy?" Renn asked. His grandson paused. "Well, you have my attention. Out with it."

"I'm the reason," Ronald said as he stepped out from behind the door molding.

"Ronald, I didn't expect we'd see you again," Renn said. "You're right, Jeremy, this can't wait. Ron, you left your post without permission. I've had guards looking for you for two days."

"So I just learned a few hours ago," Ronald replied. "When I found out, I contacted Jeremy, and he talked me into coming here. I didn't leave my post, Sir. Mr. Waterford said it was okay for me to leave and thanked me for a great job."

"He told us you deserted your post and was missing again."

"That's a lie, Sir.

"Where have you been?"

"I went to visit Mary and watch her ducks hatch. I told Mr. Waterford where I was going. I ended up staying because the ducklings were late."

Renn tried to comprehend why Cornelius lied. Was he part of the conspiracy? "Ron, can you return to the animal habitat without anyone seeing you?"

"Sure. No sweat. I made it here without getting caught."

"Good. Go back and stay with Mary. And stay out of sight until I tell you otherwise. Don't contact your friends. I want this to remain our little secret until I discover why Mr. Waterford lied."

"Commander Renn," came Jasmine's voice at 0-three hundred. "Commander, you must wake up. We have a situation." Renn remained asleep. Jasmine raised her voice two decibels. "Commander Renn, your attention is needed. Captain Xavier is on his way here."

"I'm up. I'm up," a groggy Renn stated as he bolted upright in bed. "What did you say?"

"Captain Xavier is minutes away. We have a situation."

"What kind of situation?"

"He did not say, only that it is of the highest priority."

Renn rose and shuffled to his desk, holding onto the furniture as he went. He did not do well on only four hours of sleep and a sleeping pill. A blinking red light on his control pane caught his attention. Now, what was happening? Red meant extreme danger.

"Jasmine, play recording 32-triple Z," Xavier ordered as he entered the room.

"No 'Good Morning'?" Renn asked as a video appeared in midair. It was a picture of a mysterious ship. It seemed similar to the one they spotted on radar the day before. "A red alert for that?"

"Good morning, Sir," Xavier said, reaching up and enlarging the area around the aircraft. "I have confirmed it is of the same classification as the one from yesterday. But this time, he brought friends." As the image enlarged, three more fliers appeared.

"I don't recognize their construction."

"Nor did I. Thankfully, when we rendezvoused with the fleet after the fight with the Kett, Captain Quid's escort ship gave us the latest data on new species and aircraft specifications. I located this." A picture of a hideous creature appeared on the screen. Its body was covered with various stripes of khaki green. Its head reminded Renn of a fish or eel, oval-shaped yet elongated at the back. It had no nose to speak of, only two holes above an over-enlarged mouth filled with menacing teeth. The area around the mouth contained no lips. The top jaw was a semi-circle bridge containing six molars with a canine tooth on each side. A larger, more predominant canine was to the right and left of the canines, followed by a gap and two more molars. The lower jaw was empty in the middle, designed to allow the bridge to rest when the mouth closed. On each side of the space were three long, sharp canines, a gap, followed by a smaller single canine. Positioned outside the large mouth were two curved tusks eight inches long. One was sharp, the other blunt as if broken. A small set of yellow eyes the size of a human's could be seen where the side of the face began. Its head was bald. No ears were visible. Its neck was muscular but short.

"That's a face only a mother could love." Renn walked around the desk, observing the creature from every angle. "What's it called?"

"Meet the Eli, Commander, discovered only seventy years ago. As you may have ascertained from his features, he is a flesh-eater and is not fussy about the type of meat he eats. The record indicated no home planet. It is believed this species is a nomad species that travels across the galaxy. They are dealers in the illegal market of animals used for consumption. No other trade is listed. Like the Kett, they are predators."

"I see why they are so interested in our station."

"The animals stored in our living habitat could keep them in business for centuries," Xavier commented.

"While impressive, I don't believe four aircraft require a red alert. Or a reason to wake me from my sleep."

"No, Sir, it does not. The red alert was issued when we detected a signal from our ship directed at their lead ship, and they responded."

"From our ship? Where?"

"I have the computer trying to triangulate its origins as we speak."

"Were you able to decipher the message?"

"No, the message is in a dialect not in our database or Captain Quad's. Sir, I have another reason for concern, one more sinister. I have discovered that we have an extra four beings on our ship who are not on the roster."

"What do you mean we have four extra passengers?" Renn sat down in his desk chair as the screen returned to the image of the Eli ships. "How can we have more inhabitants than we're supposed to? How does one sneak aboard my ship? Hell, we've been traveling for just under five years. Why is this just now being discovered?"

"I have no answers, Sir, except I take responsibility for this error. In my memory, I have listed every being who was or is on this ship: their names, who they are associated with, their function, and so forth. Yet, at no time did the number of inhabitants differ from the computer's data by four. It is a flaw in my subroutines, and I have corrected the error."

"Can we figure out who the four are?"

"I am comparing my data to the computers as we speak. I will discover their names. But it will take time to arrive at an answer. This ship has almost three thousand inhabitants and eleven hundred androids. Many go by various names and designations."

Renn thought for a moment. "Did your count agree with the computer's data before I brought up that group of humans?"

"You think they snuck aboard when the new arrivals came aboard?"

"It would have been the perfect time. No, that can't be right. Everyone was registered. We would have caught the discrepancy the moment they tried signing their name."

"Maybe not, Sir. A malfunction occurred in the recording process for five minutes during the registration process. Our stowaways might never have registered."

"And five minutes is enough time to slip inside and blend in."

"That it is, Sir."

Chapter 10: BABY MAMMOTH

A knock on her apartment door broke the silence in Mary's room. Setting the book she was reading on the table beside her chair, s walked over and opened the door. Standing before her was Ronald wearing a huge grin. "I thought you went to talk with my grandfather."

"I did. He wants me to stay here and lie low for a bit. He said that Mr. Waterford never told anyone he permitted me to leave. He said I went AWOL."

"Why would he say that?"

"I don't know. That's why your grandfather wants me to remain gone until he discovers the truth." Ronald lowered his eyes and shuffled his feet. "Is that invitation to crash on your couch still available?"

"Of course it is, Silly," Mary said, issuing the loner inside. "It's yours anytime you need it. But I must warn you, it's not very comfortable."

"It's got to be better than the floor. Might you have something to eat too? I never got a chance to grab something."

"Sure, help yourself to anything in the kitchen. I believe there's some vegetable lasagna in the frig and a couple of bananas. I'm off to bed. Breakfast is at 0-six hundred and thirty as usual."

The following day, after a hearty breakfast, Ron accompanied Mary to check on the ducklings. Six little fluffy yellow feathered balls were curled up asleep in a nest of hay Ron had built for them. Upon hearing footsteps, the ducklings woke and raised their heads. They hurried out of the nest and waddled over to their "parents," quacking for food.

"Hey, you're going the wrong way," Ronald chuckled when one duckling waddled toward a large suspension tank on his left.

"I think we should call that one Ronald. He's a little mixed up." Mary laughed.

Ronald rushed over and bent down to pick up the duckling. Out of the corner of his eye, he noticed movement. Three small fish were swimming in the containment tank. "Hey, Mary, I thought you said all the fish in this tank were frozen in suspended animation."

"They are, but we won't revive them until we reach New Earth."

"Well, three, no, make that five fish are swimming on the bottom. Make that eight."

"That's impossible," Mary said. She rushed to the tank. Kneeling on the floor, she peered inside, but she didn't count eight fish. There were over a hundred fish representing various species and were of different sizes. The larger fish were chasing the smaller fish in an attempt to eat them.

Mary bolted to the computer panel and checked the water temperature in the tank. It was forty-nine degrees and rising. She adjusted the controls, but it did not correct the problem. She checked on the other containers. Another three showed signs of defrosting, including the baby mammoth bio-freezer. She ran over to the sidewall and slammed the red alert button down. Red lights flashed as a loud alarm sounded.

Renn tried to stifle a yawn but to no avail. He scanned the room filled with his most trustworthy captains, commanders, and advisers. He knew all of them personally, aware of their strengths and weaknesses.

Prompted by Xavier's latest information, he summoned them to an early meeting to help him explore their options.

A soft, echoing knock filled the room as Renn tapped the wooden table. "Thank you all for interrupting your usual routines to attend this meeting. I've gathered you here to update you on the current situation and to brainstorm our next steps. Commander Oglich, can you brief us on our defense capabilities if the need arises?"

"Not the best. The station itself has no defenses. She was built as a housing unit, not a military force. She didn't need weapons when she was inside the moon. But we can defend her with the ships we have in the hangar. As I stated at the last meeting, we have restored all ships except the Command ship. And her repairs will be completed today. But we have two major problems, Sir."

"What are they?"

"Even with the restored ships, we don't have enough to mount much of a defense."

"I was under the belief that we were rebuilding our supply of fighters?" Renn inquired.

"We are, Sir," Commander Haggen answered. "But due to the main hangar serving as a temporary residence, we've had to move our construction to the smaller area below the hanger. We only have enough room there to build two ships at a time."

"How many new fighters do we have?"

"Twenty. And none have completed their testing."

How could they, Renn thought. So many pilots were lost during the battle with the Kett while trying to save Earth that there were not enough to evaluate the new fliers. "What's the second obstacle, Commander Oglich?"

"The command ship and both destroyers require the main hangar for launching. And I'm not sure if the two new cannon-ships can squeeze through the door of the lower hangar."

"In that case, we have a problem. We can't open the launch doors in the hangar without sucking every being inside out into space," Renn sighed. "And we aren't able to move them because of the instability of the station and possible new openings. How many inhabitants still occupy the hangar?"

"Four hundred and sixty-eight as of the last count," Xavier reported.

"What about pilots?" Renn asked. "Do we have enough to fly them?"

"Unknown," Commander Haggen said. "We've been training new pilots but don't have enough. It will be close."

"Perhaps we can find a few pilots amongst the new humans."

"I will conduct a sweep," Xavier said. "Master Kim, both Gerald and Dr. Kall have testified that the sphere is stable enough to be moved. Do you agree?"

"Yes, as long as you don't accelerate her too fast," Master Kim answered. "I ran another diagnostic on her this morning. She should have no problem with the tractor beams pushing her forward."

"If the station is stable enough to be moved, she is stable enough for those on the hangar floor to return to their living quarters. Xavier, I want everyone out of the hangar by twenty-two hundred tonight."

"Yes, Sir. I'll have Juaquin, I mean Jennings, start moving them."

Renn turned towards Xavier. A slip of the tongue? Xavier didn't make slips. Was it just a habit of speech? He always assigned important tasks to Juaquin. Dismissing his thought as paranoia, he pushed the idea aside.

"If everyone agrees, we will launch what fleet we have left and use them to move the station towards home at 0-eight hundred tomorrow morning. Is anyone in opposition?" No one objected. "We will proceed as planned. Now for our next problem. We planned to dispatch fliers to contact ISC. However, our visitors' arrival will make their deployment a bit more complicated than we believed. Do you have any suggestions?"

"A single flier would be a sitting duck," Captain Vin stated. "At least two fighters will need to accompany each ship."

"But that will weaken our defenses here," Command Oglich argued. "I can't recommend that."

"If you don't, it's a suicide mission. They have to …" The ceiling lights flashed red as a warning sounded. "Now what?"

"I am getting reports that there is a problem in the Habitat Sphere," Xavier announced.

"A problem? What kind of problem?" Renn asked.

"Certain containers have lost power. The specimens are defrosting."

"Meeting dismissed," Renn shouted as he rose and prepared to leave. Xavier grabbed his arm.

"Where do you think you're going, Sir?"

"To the Habitat Sphere. Where else?"

"Sir, you're not Captain Renn anymore. You're the Head Commander. Your place is on the bridge, awaiting word from your captains and me on what transpires."

"The hell it is," Renn said, pulling his arm out of Xavier's grasp. "My granddaughter's in that sphere. That's where I belong."

"I thought you might say that. Ricardo will meet us in hallway 3-B2 with a motorized cart." Renn lips tightened. "You can't run all the way to the Habitat Sphere, Renn. Remember what happened last time you ran somewhere?"

Renn's look intensified as he ground his teeth.

"Plus, we can use the air tubes and arrive in fifteen minutes versus the hour it would take you to walk it, providing you even made it."

"You and I must have a discussion regarding my heart and what I can and can't do," Renn replied.

"Yes, Sir. I have discussed this with every commander since becoming Head Security Captain." Renn was sure he witnessed Xavier smirking.

————————

When Renn and Xavier arrived at the Containment House, it was chaos. Scientists, workers, and robots were running everywhere, shouting orders, trying to stop the cascade of failing storage containers.

"Grandpa," Mary shouted as she raced to Renn. "Some containers are failing, and their contents are thawing. The animals inside are waking up."

"Are you okay?"

"Yes, I'm fine, but they're not. We have to do something."

Movement in the tank behind Mary caught Renn's attention. He drew closer. His eyes opened white as he witnessed hundreds of minnows swimming erratically, zipping from side to side. Above them, larger fish hung suspended in a semi-liquid mixture, squirming to get free. It was no surprise the smaller fish were frantic – they were about to become dinner.

"Are any of the larger animals coming out of cryonic sleep?"

"I don't know," Mary stated. "I pushed the alarm button as soon as we realized there was a problem. I haven't had time to check any of the other containers."

"We?"

"Ronald and me. It was Ronald who discovered the freed fish."

Renn searched the field of faces for Ronald. "Where is he?"

"He's hiding in the back. You told him not to be seen."

"Yes, I did. Now, who's in charge of this facility?"

"What? I can't hear you over the alarms?" Mary stated.

"Xavier, can you do something about these alarms and lights?" The blaring sound stopped. Renn turned and stared at Xavier.

"What? You wanted them off. I'm connected to the ship and did as you asked." There was that smirk again. "Professor Williams is in charge of this facility. Would you like me to find her?"

"I think I have an easier way. Everyone, stop for a moment," Renn shouted. But his words were drowned in the ocean of a thousand sounds.

Xavier gave a shrill whistle that made everyone, human and alien, halt and cringe in pain. "Everyone shut up and stop what you're doing. The Head Commander wants to talk to you."

"We really need to have that talk," Renn said. "Is there a Professor, a Professor ..." Renn leaned over to Xavier. "What's his name again?"

"Her name is Professor Williams."

"Is Professor Williams here?" Renn shouted.

"I'm right here," a female voice said from the back. A tall, petite female ran forward, her hand waving. "I'm Professor Williams."

Renn just stared for a moment, his mouth partially open. Except for His Jenny, he had never seen a more beautiful woman. She had red curly hair with tiny streaks of gray showing through. Her eyes were the bluest he had ever seen. Little freckles dotted her cheeks.

"You might want to close your mouth and stop staring," Xavier whispered.

"What, oh yes. Professor Williams. What's the status?"

"We have twenty-six units malfunctioning. Fifteen of the containers house spores, fungi, seeds, and tubulars. Since they do not require being frozen, we can manage them with little problem. Eleven units contain animals. Thanks to Mary's early warning, we were able to reroute power to eight of the units. But we've had no luck with the remaining four."

"What do they hold?" Renn asked.

"Two contain sperm, eggs, zygotes, and fetuses from a hundred and two extinct species. If we lose them, they are gone forever. The third is the tank that Mary discovered. My crew is getting the larger fish out before they revive and start snacking on the smaller fish."

"Something I am sure those little guys will be grateful for," Renn chuckled. "They appear a little nervous."

Professor Williams did not laugh. "The last unit is the one that contains our baby mammoth. I don't think I have to tell you what a loss that will be when we lose her."

"Can you take us to the unit?"

"This way." Professor Williams pushed through the crowd. Mary, Renn, and Xavier followed.

"Professor, you said when we lost her. Do you expect her to die?"

"For some reason, her unit didn't simply malfunction. The temperature inside the freezer rose within minutes, causing her to begin thawing within minutes. With her body encased in cryonic gel, we can't assist her, free her, or refreeze her. At this rate of revitalization, her cells will explode, and her heart will stop within ten minutes."

"If you can free her from the cryogenic liquid, could you save her?" Xavier asked.

"It might be possible. We could pack the baby in ice and reduce her inner body temperature. Once she was stable, we could raise her body temperature over the next week. But there's no way to extract her."

The baby mammoth was suspended in a block resembling ice. Everything from her front legs back remained held in the frozen trap, and everything from her front legs forward hung outside the icy liquid. As they neared, her trunk quivered. But it was her eyes that caught Renn's attention. They were wide, filled with terror as she hung suspended, unable to break free. Her breathing was troubled. Pinkish foam dripped from the corners of her mouth.

"Can't we do anything to free her?" Renn asked.

"Not unless you want to die, too," Professor Williams answered. "That liquid encasing her would turn our hands into frozen popsicles in seconds. Upon hitting the ground, our limbs would break and smash into pieces."

"She keeps looking at me," Ronald said as he emerged from the other side. She reached out with her tiny trunk twice, begging me to help her."

"This was the one animal I wanted to restore more than any other," Professor Williams stated, tears slipping onto her cheeks. "Now, I wish we had never found her."

Renn said in a high-pitched giggle. "I, too, said the mammoth." He cleared his throat and hoped no one noticed his nervous giggle.

Xavier glanced inquisitively at the Head Commander inquisitively, then stopped, extending his arm to permit an android with an armful of metal bars to pass. "Is this iggium?"

"Yes, Captain. We use it to reinforce the sidewalls of some containers."

"Today, it's going to save that baby's life. Don't move." Grabbing one of the bars from the pile, Xavier jammed it as hard as possible into the frozen liquid behind the mammoth's front legs. The impact caused only a tiny crack. Xavier hit it again. A second crack spread through the ice. On his third try, the bar shattered into a thousand frozen pieces. But the bar had done its job – a sizeable chunk behind the mammoth's right leg fell to the floor. The baby slipped down a half-inch. Xavier grabbed another bar and hit the block, breaking off another piece.

Seeing what his commander was trying to do, the android dropped the last two pieces of iggium. He grabbed a bar and smashed it into the area Xavier had been hitting. Another large chunk broke free, allowing the mammoth to slip even further down..

"Bring me more iggium," Xavier shouted. Six androids rushed forward with more bars and tackled the foe before them.

When he realized Xavier's plan would work, Renn said, "Mary, find a cart to put her on."

Mary left and returned as the block split, dropping the baby mammoth onto the floor.

"No one touch her," Professor Williams shouted. "She's still covered in cryonics juice."

"We can't just let her die," Ron cried.

"No, we cannot," Xavier said. Before anyone could stop him, he lifted the two-hundred-pound baby. Carrying her against his chest, he placed her on the cart. As he stood, pieces of his uniform fell to the floor, shattering upon impact, destroyed by the cryogenic liquid dripping from the mammoth's hair. Xavier's skin on his chest and arm, where the mammoth had rested against his, was discolored and hung in strips of dead gray flesh. Experiencing stiffness in his right arm, he flexed his fingers to regain circulation. The sound of two bones breaking inside his arm resonated in his ear. Xavier thought two broken bones were a reasonable price to pay for the life of an extinct mammoth.

"Captain, how did you do that? That liquid should have ended you," Professor Williams stated.

"Never underestimate the strength of an android," Renn replied, pushing Xavier towards the door.

"No," Professor Williams stated, blocking the two from leaving. She reached down and grabbed Xavier's injured arm, inspecting his injuries. "That arm should have shattered. It has third-degree burns, but I believe it is salvable."

"Professor, I don't have time to debate what you think you know about androids," Renn stated in an authoritative voice. "My captain needs medical attention right away. I expect your status report to be on my desk within an hour. Mary, keep an eye on Ronald for me." Renn turned and escorted Xavier to the cart. "That was a dangerous thing to do in front of her. How did you carry that mammoth without breaking into a million pieces?"

"I told you, Commander, I am special."

Secrets, Renn thought. More secrets.

Chapter 11: A GENTLE PUSH

"Dr. Chi is the one who should do your repairs," Master Kim stated as he cut off the dead skin on Xavier's arm. After removing four tiny screws, he prided open the arm panel. Two shattered bones lay inside. "Dr. Chi is the expert on repairing androids. It's been years since I've worked on one."

"You are Master Tii's great-great-grandson," Xavier replied. "He was my creator, and he passed my secrets on to you. You have what I need. Dr. Chi does not."

Master Kim walked to a nearby cabinet and removed a plain wooden box. He returned it to the table where Xavier waited and opened it. Inside was a collection of fifteen android bones made of pure briiddium, the strongest alloy in the known universe.

"Had my great-great-grandfather been aware of your recklessness, he might have left us more replacements. My supply is getting sparse. At the rate you go through them, you may have to make the thousand-year journey to your place of origin for more parts."

"Perhaps one day, but I shall rely on your little wooden box of secret parts for now."

"Yes, secrets." Master Kim meticulously removed the broken pieces from within Xavier's arm. Using a water gun, he flushed the area to remove any lingering fragments, then dried it with an air gun. "I will have to replace your secondary vein in this arm." Tying off the ends of the secondary vein, he cut out the damaged piece.

Retrieving a section of vein tubing from a drawer, he inserted the replacement inside the existing vein and sealed both ends with a special android glue that he also kept in his secret box. "That should work. Avoid any strenuous activity for three days. No more hero acts. Give this adhesive time to glue your parts together."

"When can I use my arm?"

"If you go easy, you can use it in two hours. And I was serious, Xavier. No strenuous activity. Is that clear?"

"Yes."

"I mean it, Xavier."

"I will restrict my activities for the three days."

"Now, let's replace those broken bones." Master Kim hunted through the box and selected two bones to use. First, he removed the severed humerus and replaced it with a new bone by attaching it to the ligaments with screws and adhesive. He next removed the shattered ulna.

"You're lucky that cryogenics fluid only shattered your ulna. It could have broken all your arm's bones into a million pieces," Master Kim said. Using a pair of tweezers, he removed tiny pieces of broken bone. He placed the new bone beside the arm and discovered it was four millimeters too long. "Looks like I'm running short on needed lengths. Another reason to stop needing repairs." He shaved the bone down to the proper length using a hand grinder. As with the humerus bone, he connected the adjusted ulna with screws and adhesive. "Okay, now sit here for ten minutes. No moving anything, not even your fingers."

Xavier counted down the minutes. The moment the clock registered ten minutes, Xavier yelled, "Can I move my arm now?"

"Try moving your fingers first." Master Kim watched the android flex his fingers. He inspected the joined edges of the tubing and witnessed no leakage.

"As good as new."

"I doubt that. Now, your arm? Raise it up and down slowly?"

"Working fine." Xavier raised his injured arm above his head and back down. "No one will ever know I was injured."

"Renn does, as do a few others who were present." Master Kim closed the panel on the arm. He reached over and grabbed a sling.

"What's that for?" Xavier asked. "I hope you don't expect me to wear that."

"I said it needed three days to heal, which means it needs to remain stationary. So, Xavier, you have a choice. You can wear the sling and go about your usual duties or stay in the infirmary for the next three days "

"You never make things easy, do you, Master Kim?"

Master Kim snickered. "Don't blame me for your idiotic moves. So, sling or infirmary."

"The sling."

"It doesn't look bad," Master Kim said as he placed the wrap around the android's neck. Maybe you'll make a new fashion statement."

"Ha, ha, hilarious."

Master Kim laughed. "By the way, now that your friend Renn is Head Commander, have you told him your secrets?"

"A few. As with Commander Glogg, I will inform the new Head Commander as it becomes necessary. Not before."

"Does he know you are one of only two androids capable of hiding secrets? And that you two are the only two of your kind?"

"Even though Commander Renn has always thought of me as another life form and not artificial intelligence, I doubt he could control his fear if he were aware of what my sister and I are capable of. AIs are safe because they cannot lie; they have no secrets. If the truth were known, they would fear us, and all possibility of coexistence would end."

"Commander Renn must realize you are not like other androids."

"Yes. I've mentioned to him numerous times that I am different. He knows my unidentified sister is different, too. But he does not fathom how different we are. Plus, she was not activated for centuries after I came online, so he perceives no connection between us. It was not until Renn needed her that you awakened her."

"He was so devastated when he learned of his wife's death. I never met anyone who grieved for another as he did. I did not doubt that activating Jenny was the right thing to do. But if you keep pulling stunts as you did with the mammoth, he and others will realize the truth."

"Not all of it."

Master Kim paused. "Why did you save that mammoth, Xavier? That is not a programmed response."

"I do not know why. I just couldn't let her die."

"My great-great-grandfather gave you the capacity to experience emotions. They have risen in the past. Are they intensifying?"

"I believe so. That poor animal was hanging there, struggling to survive. She was so scared. My heart hurt for some reason, and my eyes were full of tears. Perhaps I am malfunctioning."

"No, you're growing as all life forms do."

"But I'm not a life form."

"I'm not so sure about that." Master Kim replaced the cover on Xavier's arm, hiding what lay inside once more. "I don't have any skin coverings here. You'll have to have Dr. Chi do that part of the repair on your arm and replace the lost skin on your chest. And he'll have to replace the dead skin on your chest. That's going to be a major repair. In the meantime, I can use the synthetic material we use on the ship to cover your chest wound. It won't look pretty, but it will be sufficient until Dr. Chi completes the needed repairs. You'll find a fresh shirt on the hook behind the door to wear until you can retrieve one of your own."

"Yeah, I kind of destroyed the shirt I had on." Xavier retrieved the shirt from the hook and slipped it on. Xavier turned and smiled. "See, like I said, as good as new."

"Yet, by the look on your face, something is still wrong."

"With all that's been going on with the station and Jenny being ill, I've been trying to answer the question of why Master Tii made Jenny and me. What is our purpose?"

"That answer I do not have. If my grandfather told me, I don't recall. Remember, I was only ten years of age when he died. In the journals he left behind, he merely stated you were both built to prevent a travesty in the future."

"What kind of travesty?"

"He didn't say."

"Will we do it together, or do we each have our own travesty to stop?"

"Again, he did not say." Master Kim closed the wooden box and returned it to its hiding place in the cupboard. "Now, both of our secrets are safe once more."

"How's the arm?" Renn asked as Xavier entered the bridge's Briefing Room dressed in a new uniform and wearing a sling around his neck.

"I'm repaired and ready for duty. I told you there would be no permanent damage."

"Are you sure? I don't consider wearing a sling as confirmation that you are ready for duty. Did Dr. Chi give you a release to return to duty?"

"It was only some minor repairs. The sling is just a cautionary measure. I assure you, I am fine." Xavier reached out for the report in Renn's hand. "May I see Professor Williams' report? "

"Xavier, you are well versed in protocols. You were injured and, therefore, must be released for duty."

"What does her report say?"

"Xavier, where's the release?"

The android reached into his pocket and pulled out a piece of paper. "Here is my medical release from Master Kim. If you are now happy, perhaps you will answer my question."

"Master Kim? I thought you were going to Dr. Chi for repairs?" Renn asked.

"Dr. Chi does not have the necessary equipment to repair an android bone. Only Master Km has such a capability."

"I did not know that." Renn read the report. "Xavier, Master Kim's report states that you not only broke your humerus but shattered your ulna as well."

"It also says I can return to duty, but I am restricted on my activities and must keep my arm in the protective sling for the next ten hours."

"Yes, it does. Given this new information, I believe you would do better to rest until tomorrow in your quarters."

"Please, Renn, I cannot remain inactive for ten hours. If I remain on the bridge, I can fulfill Master Kim's instructions to a higher degree. In my quarters, I can guarantee you my arm will be out of this sling in less than an hour. I ask you again, Commander, what species did Professor Williams lose?"

"Xavier, what about the arm?"

Xavier glared at his commander, one of the few times Renn could remember the android giving him one. "Sir, all you need to know is that my arm is repaired. How and where is not something I am comfortable revealing. I am fit for duty. That should be sufficient."

If Xavier did not want to answer, pursuing this line of questioning would be unproductive. Xavier guarded his secrets well. "Can you at least tell me how you survived the cryonic gel?"

"You know the answer to that question, Renn."

"You are special."

"See, you do learn."

"I am glad you are! I can't imagine life aboard this ship without your presence and assistance." Xavier did not comment. Renn sighed. Sometimes, androids were so infuriating. "As for Professor William's species, we lost the totoaba, a fish from the upper Gulf of California. The totoaba, a fish from the upper Gulf of California, became extinct because of illegal fishing for its swim bladder, which was once valued at over four thousand dollars a pound in China.

"Why?'

"They said it cured illnesses."

"But a fish's swim bladder would not affect diseases."

"The Chinese used many animal parts for medicinal, including elephant tusks, rhino horns, swiftlet's nests, water buffalo parts, and sea horses."

"To drive a species to extinction for a believed medical treatment makes no sense."

"Whoever said humans made sense?"

"True. Professor Williams reports that the freezer that held the mammoth is unrestorable and that two other empty containers have malfunctioned."

"Since Master Kim was busy repairing you, he hasn't been able to examine the faulty freezers," Renn said. "But he sent a team, and they reported intentional sabotage of those containers."

"Did they know why?"

"No, but it was deliberate. Considering this development, we should advance our plans to move the station."

"I agree. With this sabotage and the new threat of the Eli, we have no choice. Plus, we cannot house a growing mammoth aboard the station. According to the professor's report, it is too dangerous to put her back into cryonics for at least a year, by which time she will be grown.

Renn raised his arms and stretched as he envisioned a full-grown mammoth wreaking havoc on the station. "You're sure you're up to being on the bridge?"

"I assure you I am okay."

"Alright, I'm out of here. I'm calling it a day, going home, seeing My Jenny, and enjoying a tasty supper for a change. Tomorrow is a big day."

"How is Jenny doing?"

"She sleeps. Sometimes, I fear she will never awaken." Renn stood, grabbing his reports to take home. "Is the main hangar empty?"

"All residents were reassigned to new living arrangements or returned home. Commander Oglich has raised the Command Ship and the two destroyers to the departure level. He decided not to launch the new double-cannon ship since it only had two flights. We have refueled the fliers, and they will launch at 0-six hundred tomorrow morning, along with the larger vessels. At 0-seven hundred thirty, a station-wide announcement will advise all residents to stay clear of the outer walls. At 0-seven hundred forty-five, Master Kim will erect a force field around the entire station. At 0-eight hundred, if Master Kim and Commander Jen agree, the fleet will turn on their tractor beams and nudge the space station forward."

"We will meet at 0-six hundred thirty. Are you still comparing the resident rooster with our current inhabitants?"

"The inhabitants aboard this station have called themselves by many names and variations of those names. The comparison has taken more time than I expected. It should be completed within the next eight hours."

"Do me a favor – don't wake me up in the middle of the night unless we need to take immediate action. I'd like one night of peaceful sleep."

———————

Renn reread Master Kim and Professor Williams' reports over dinner. Tonight, everyone had things to do, so he dined alone, which was okay with him. It gave him time to reevaluate what was going on. A whiff of her cologne drifted into his nostrils when he lifted Professor Williams' report. He took deep breaths, once again surprised at her beauty's impact on him.

At twenty hundred hours, he kissed Jenny good night and retired for the evening. He was anxious about tomorrow and their attempt to move the station. He feared sleep would not be attainable, but when Jasmine announced it was time to rise, he was delighted to discover he had slept through the night. He wondered if Xavier had discovered who their saboteurs were.

"Good morning, Dad," Sarina greeted as Renn entered the dining room. "Xavier asked me to inform you that everything is proceeding as planned, and he will meet you in the hangar at 0-six hundred and thirty." She placed a plate of bacon, hash browns, and basted eggs in front of him, along with toast.

"Am I dying today or something? I seldom am giving this for breakfast anymore."

Sarina laughed. "You've got a big day ahead of you. Mom told me she always served you this on such days to start on a pleasant note. I just thought I'd continue her tradition for her."

"That she did. Somehow, she always sensed when I needed something special." He glanced towards their bedroom. His heart ached to talk with her again.

After downing two cups of coffee and finishing his breakfast, Renn walked to the bridge, having trouble keeping his gate below a full run. He wasn't sure if it was the exceptional breakfast or the adrenaline rush of possibly learning who the culprits were that put the extra zip in his step. The moment he entered the hangar, he walked straight to Xavier.

"Good morning, Commander. It appears you had a most restful sleep last night."

"Do you have my report?" Renn asked, not wanting to play niceties.

"Yes, but I want to double-check my findings. I must be sure."

"Xavier, when have you ever been wrong?"

"Never."

"Since you're never wrong, TELL ME." The people nearby glanced in Renn's direction, surprised by the loudness of the Commander's voice. "Tell me," Renn whispered.

Xavier examined the faces on the bridge. While he trusted everyone there, what he had to say was for the Commander's ears only. "Follow me, Sir." Xavier led the Commander to the Head Commander's lounge. Once inside, he whispered the answer.

"Are you sure?"

"I find no record in the database on these four. They must be our perpetrators. I have all four working on a special assignment with three guards. When we activate the force field at 0-seven hundred forty-five, it will also surround them."

"Shouldn't we arrest them?"

"When the station moves forward, their actions will testify to their guilt or innocence. If they try to interfere or contact their counterparts out in space, I will be certain we have the ones responsible for our dilemma."

"And if they don't?"

"I'll have to come up with another plan."

"If they are our culprits, can they impede this morning's activities?"

"No. The force field configuration allows a transmission to be received inside the room. However, one cannot be sent back out."

"Ingenious."

Xavier furrowed his right brows, creating a deep line on his forehead. "When catching rats, the catch rate is higher if you allow the vermin to taste the bait before springing the trap."

"How true," Renn chuckled. "I recommend we return to the bridge."

"Agreed." The two slipped out of the room. Renn took his seat in the Commander's chair.

"Sir, Commander Oglich reports all ships are in position and ready when we are," Captain Uhl announced.

"Issue the station-wide warning," Xavier ordered.

A message broadcasted across the station advised the inhabitants of what would transpire. It stated that everyone needed to remain at least twenty feet from any outside wall unless they wished to suffer bodily harm.

"Master Kim, enact the force field," Renn ordered.

"Aye, Sir." Master Kim entered his code into the panel. A slight humming filled the air as Master Kim entered his code, causing a vertical glowing red line of light to spread across the outside wall. As it grew, the lights on the bridge dimmed.

"Master Kim, do we have a problem?"

"Not yet, Sir. The field is draining more power than I anticipated."

"Reduce lighting across the station by 18 hemps," Renn ordered. "Cut power to all nonessential areas."

"Aye, Sir."

They waited fifteen minutes as the force field expanded, stretching across the station's exterior. The station groaned and creaked under the strain.

"How are we doing?"

"She's two-thirds complete. Just a few more minutes."

Unable to sit still, Renn stood and paced in a tight circle around the control panel where Master Kim worked. Would the shield hold? Would the ship remain intact? Renn glanced at his watch. O-seven hundred thirty-eight. They were eight minutes ahead of schedule.

Finally, Ensign Mack made the announcement Renn had been awaiting. "Force shield complete and holding, Sir."

A. "What's her status?"

"All stations report she is stable and shows no signs of strain or distress. We're a go for Operation Forward."

"Commander Jen, are you in agreement?"

"Operations agrees with Master Kim. We are a go for Operation Forward."

"Commander Uhl, advise Commander Oglich to proceed with the tractor beams at his discretion."

Renn's heart hammered in his chest, a frantic drum solo against his ribs. He stood frozen before the viewing screen on Master Kim's console, his gaze locked on the single needle that held the key to their fate. It lay motionless, a tauntingly still sliver against the dark surface. Five agonizing minutes crawled by. Renn dared not breathe, convinced even the slightest movement would disrupt the delicate balance needed for the needle to flicker to life. A bead of sweat trickled down his temple, the tension in the room thick enough to choke on.

Finally, unable to bear the silence any longer, he choked out the question, his voice barely a whisper, "Isn't it working?"

"It may take a while for her to start moving," Master Kim reported. "The fleet will start with a weak beam and increase the intensity once they know it is safe. From my estimates, I predict the needle will move in eighteen more minutes."

Eighteen minutes seemed more like eighteen hours, but the needle finally moved. It continued to rise.

"She's being repelled," Master Kim announced. "She is moving forward at a velocity of point seven-two rams. Two-point eight. Five-point three. Eight-point zero. Ten-point one. Fleet has stopped increasing the intensity of the beam."

Xavier stood beside him, his face devoid of expression as he pointed a finger at the radar screen. A faint blip, representing their ship, wobbled ever so slightly away from the designated course on the display. "She's drifting a little off course," Xavier said.

"Captain Vin, we're detecting a misalignment of approximately two degrees off our intended heading," the navigation officer reported crisply. "Recommend a forty-eight till course correction to compensate."

As the captain relayed the order, the station's port-side fliers intensified their tractor beam output. The increased gravitonic force gently nudged the massive station back into proper alignment, and its trajectory was now accurate.

"Course correction complete," the officer confirmed with a nod. "We're back on track, Captain."

"Our second biggest hurdle passed," Renn sighed.

For the next hour, all eyes remained fixed on the screens. Minor trajectory adjustments were made twice, and the space station accepted them without objection.

Xavier's communicator beeped. After reading the message, he walked over to the commander. "Sir, our friends just received a message from our visitors."

"Master Kim, Captain Vin, please give your crew a 'job well done' from me. Extend to Commander Oglich a special thank you. I have a matter that needs my attention. Please keep me apprised of what transpires."

"Gual, I'm getting a signal from the lead ship. They're awaiting instructions."

Cornelius strode purposefully across the floor, his boots ringing against the deck plating. Halting before the speaker, he fixed the offender with a stern glare. His hand lashed out without warning, delivering a stinging slap that echoed through the hushed room. "I've told you not to call me that while aboard this ship," he growled, jaw clenched. "My designation is Cornelius, Cornelius Waterford."

The struck officer recoiled, raising a hand to his reddened cheek. "I forgot for a second," the man replied, rubbing his face. "It won't happen again."

Straightening his suit, Cornelius leveled a warning look at each crew member. "See that it doesn't happen again," he growled. "We're so close to our goal."

Turning to Sam, Cornelius barked, "Contact the ship and advise them Commander Renn will attempt to move the station. When he does, our comrades might have a chance to take out some of their fliers and cripple their defenses even more."

"Yes, Sir." Sam's fingers danced across the encrypted comm channel, relaying the message. Cornelius allowed himself a thin smile. Their audacious plan was finally coming to fruition after years of meticulous preparation.

Cornelius clanked across the floor as he waited, stopping after three minutes of silence. "Well, what is their response?"

"There isn't one," Sam reported. "I don't know if our signal is getting out."

"We've never had trouble before," Cornelius bellowed, grabbing the communicator from the man's hands. "What's wrong with this thing?"

"Perhaps something in this room is preventing our message from being transmitted," Charles suggested.

"Paul, go into the hallway and, if clear, send a signal out," Cornelius ordered.

Paul hurried towards the exit, his heart pounding with urgency. But as he reached the exit, an unyielding barrier blocked his path. Frowning, he placed his hands on the door panel and pulled with all his might, but the unforgiving metal refused to budge. "Sir, the door won't open."

"What do you mean it won't open?" Cornelius growled. He strode over, brow furrowed in confusion. Putting his shoulder into opening the barrier, he grunted with effort. But the door remained infuriatingly sealed, denying them release no matter how he strained against it. Stepping back, Cornelius wiped the sweat from his brow as realization dawned. "There must be a malfunction on the ship."

The two men exchanged a loaded glance, their predicament settling heavily upon them. Trapped within these unforgiving walls, cut off from the rest of the crew, they could only imagine the severity of the issue plaguing the ship's systems. As the silence stretched, the muffled thrum of the engines seemed to take on an ominous tone. Whatever malfunction occurred, it didn't bode well for their mission or survival.

Paul's fists pounded against the unyielding door in a desperate rhythm. "Hey! Can anyone hear me?" he shouted, his voice strained.

"Save your energy. No one's going to hear you," Cornelius said, his voice level despite the direness of their situation. He placed a firm hand on Paul's shoulder, halting the younger man's frantic pounding. Paul opened his mouth to protest, but Cornelius shook his head. "Someone's bound to stop by to check on our progress and set us free. In the meantime, we might as well keep working."

For a tense moment, Paul was ready to argue. His shoulders slumped in resignation as the logic of Cornelius' words sank in. "You're right. We need to stay focused."

Every groan of the ship, every flicker of the dying light, seemed amplified in the cramped space. After five hours, exhaustion finally claimed even Cornelius' forced optimism. He slumped against the wall with a heavy sigh, his breath echoing in the silence. "Alright, that's it for now," he rasped, his voice hoarse.

"Why is it so hot in here?" Charles asked, wiping beads of sweat from his brow with his hand. Walking over to the environmental controls, he squinted at the readout. His stomach dropped. "Ninety-five degrees," he muttered in disbelief. "That explains why it's so stinky hot in here." Rapidly fanning himself, Charles tapped a few commands into the console, but no matter which sequence he tried, the numbers remained defiantly high. "The ventilation system isn't working either."

The stale air hung thick and oppressive, each breath a struggle. Cornelius dragged a forearm across his damp brow, his expression hardening. "That's just fantastic. As if being trapped wasn't bad enough."

The lights dimmed by half. "Must be a drainage on the system."

"Maybe the move went bad," Paul commented. "What if something catastrophic happened, and everyone's dead except for us?"

"Don't be dumb, Paul," Cornelius chastised. "I'm sure it was necessary to turn off non-essential areas. In the excitement of moving the sphere, they forgot we were down here. Once they realize their error, someone will come and get us."

"And if no one does?"

"If no one returns by tomorrow morning, we'll break through the outside wall and leave. Since we can't work in this light, let's get some sleep." As the four slept, no one noticed the communicator blinking, their alien comrades asking for instructions.

Chapter 12: THE SECRET FREEZER

"Do you think our four stowaways have mellowed enough?" Renn asked Xavier.

"I believe the heat, lack of air, no food, dim lights, and imprisonment should have done the trick, Sir."

"What of our outside visitors?"

"Three ships left at 0-one hundred. The lead ship remained until 0-five hundred. None have returned."

"I bet they're having a heck of a time trying to figure out what happened," Renn said as he stood. "Let's go see what our stowaways have to say."

"I wish to stop by the medical unit and get Dr. Robinson. I want an analysis done on the four to determine their identity."

"You don't think they're human?"

"It is a possibility. There are species across the universe who look remarkably like humans. Without a keen eye or a medical analysis, one could not tell the difference."

"There's no way that creature in the picture you showed me of the Eli could pass as human."

"It is possible that someone altered these men to look like humans."

"Could they be AIs?"

"Androids? I highly doubt that. Androids are too intelligent to have been caught so easily."

Renn laughed and shook his head. "You do think highly of yourself, don't you?"

"No, Sir. I am just stating the obvious."

———————

At 0-eight hundred and thirty hours, the lights and cooling generators turned on in the room housing the four unknowns. Cornelius tried the door again and found that it was still locked. But with the other systems operating, he was confident their confinement would soon end.

Thirty-six minutes later, the front door opened. Xavier, Commander Renn, and four androids entered.

"Boy, are we glad to see you," Paul shouted, a big smile on his face. "We feared everyone got blown up or something, and we were the only ones alive."

"Paul feared that," Cornelius stated, annoyed by his subordinate's display. "I figured it was a simple malfunction or power-down.

"Actually, neither," Renn said. "Why don't we all have a seat at the table, and I'll explain." A fifth android entered, pushing a cart of food." I figured you must be starving and brought you something to eat."

"Thanks," Cornelius said as he and the others took seats. "We haven't eaten since lunch yesterday." Cornelius noticed the four androids, each taking a position behind him and the other three, as he served himself a bowl of oatmeal. He sat his spoon down and stared at the Commander. "Is there a problem?"

"You tell me," Renn replied.

"I don't know what you mean?"

"Might I inquire where you received your engineering degree?"

"IT Tech. It's in my file."

"Funny. There is no Cornelius Waterford listed as ever attending IT Tech." Renn was bluffing. They could not verify whether Cornelius had attended IT Tech. He hoped Cornelius did not realize that.

"There must be some mistake."

"Yes, there is. The mistake is you thinking you could stow away on my station and not get caught. You are not listed on the roster."

The left side of Cornelius's mouth twitched ever so slightly. "Okay, you got us. We weren't with the group chosen to come aboard. We didn't want to die on Earth. An opportunity presented itself to steal away with a group being brought up, and we took it. It's not a crime to want to live."

"But it is a crime to stow away," Xavier said as he neared the imposter. "And it is a crime to sabotage this station and conspire with possible hostile aliens." Xavier nodded, and the soldier behind Cornelius grabbed his two arms and pinned them to the table. The stowaway struggled against the force of the android's hold, twisting his arms and trying to break their hold. Xavier through Cornelius' clothing and double checked his pockets in search for hidden items. "Well, well, what do I have here?" Xavier lifted a communications device out of a small pocket hidden inside his shirt. "Could this be how you've been corresponding with the Eli?"

"I don't know what you're talking about," Cornelius said.

"Dr. Robinson, if you would," Renn said.

Cornelius' eyes narrowed, and he clenched his jaw when the doctor walked in with a medical bag. "What's he doing here?"

"Not only do I not believe your story, but I also don't believe you're human," Renn replied. "Dr. Robinson is here to do a little test to determine if I am wrong or right."

Cornelius desperately struggled against the strength of the android. The android strengthened his grip as he did, almost cutting off the circulation to Cornelius' hands.

Dr. Robinson ran his medical tricorder over the suspected alien. "Could be human, might not. I will need a blood and tissue sample to be sure. I can check the blood here, but I'll need to do the tissue analysis back at my lab." He withdrew a syringe from his bag and jabbed it into Cornelius' arm, withdrawing a tube of blood. "The best part for a tissue analysis is at the base of the neck where the hair follicles begin." Without a word, Xavier shoved Cornelius' head forward until it hit the table. Dr. Robinson removed a small piece of tissue with hair follicles. He placed it in a container and put it in the bag. He prepared a slide of Cornelius' blood and examined it in his portable reader.

"Well, Doc?" Renn asked.

"Not human. Not synthetic either. An alien life form I have not encountered before."

Xavier grabbed Cornelius' hair and yanked the imposter's head up. "Who are you? What are you? Why are those ships stalking us? Why did you sabotage this station?"

"I have nothing to say." Cornelius gave the android a look of pure hate.

"Doc, make sure you get samples from the other three," Renn ordered. The androids behind each prisoner secured their hands to the table while Xavier walked around and slammed their foreheads forward.

Like Cornelius' sample, Paul and Charles' blood and hair samples revealed they were not human. Paul's tests showed he was a hundred percent human.

"How did you get mixed up with this scum?" Renn asked.

"Keep your mouth shut," Cornelius shouted.

"I, I." Paul looked first at Renn, then at Cornelius. The threat of vengeance filled Cornelius' eyes. "I have nothing to say."

"I think we can rectify that." Xavier smiled. "Shall I have them taken to the holding cell, Sir?"

"Is the hangar still void of beings?"

"Yes, Sir. There's no one on the hangar floor at this moment."

"Let's take them there. Maybe our stowaways will feel more like talking in a larger room." Yanked to their feet, the four were quickly handcuffed behind their backs and forcefully dragged down the corridors to the hangar." The soldiers lined them up facing the hangar door.

"Does anyone have anything to say before we begin this interrogation?" Renn asked. Everyone was silent, but Paul was barely holding it together. Charles looked a little nervous as well. "Xavier, they are all yours."

"You're wasting your time," Cornelius spat as Xavier dragged him before an escape door.

"I don't believe so. If you do not tell me what I want to know, I will place you inside that door. You will have thirty seconds to answer my question before I hit this red button. When I push it, the button will expel you into space. Within three seconds, you will freeze and asphyxiate."

"You're bluffing," Cornelius said. "Androids can't murder sentient beings."

"Oh, that's where you're wrong," Renn said as he approached the suspected Eli. "In matters of aggression, our androids have complete control over us. They can extinguish any foe who endangers this ship."

"You're lying."

"You know I'm not. I am sure you have heard a story or two during your stay with us of androids executing people. It doesn't matter the species; They are not discriminatory." Renn turned and took five steps toward the exit before stopping. "What is your purpose here?"

Cornelius remained silent.

"One last time. What is your purpose here?"

Again, nothing.

Xavier opened the escape door, shoved the handcuffed alien inside, and closed the door. With his hand over the red button, he announced, "You have five seconds. Five, four, three, two, one." Xavier activated the button, forcefully expelling the alien outside, causing its demise. "Who's next?" The android grabbed Charles. "What is your purpose here?"

"I have nothing to say to you, you hunk of metal." Charles spat at the android.

Xavier shoved Charles inside the escape door as he wiped the spittle from his face. He gave the prisoner the same options. When he didn't answer, Xavier pushed the red button.

"Which one should I take next?"

"Take Paul," Renn suggested. "He appears willing to go."

Xavier walked over and grabbed the trembling human. Immediately, Paul fell to the floor, sobbing and shaking in fear. "No, please."

"If you don't want to die, tell me what I want to know," Xavier shouted.

"I can't."

Xavier shoved him inside the door and held his hand over the red button. He noticed that the man was so scared he had peed himself. "Five, four, three, two . . ."

"Stop," Paul screamed. "I'll tell you everything you want to know."

Xavier opened the door and yanked Paul out. "Take this piece of filth down to the interrogation room. See that he's given something to eat and drink." Xavier waited until Paul was out of the room. "Take the other three prisoners to the holding cell and keep them well guarded."

"Should we provide them with food and drink also?" one of the guards asked.

"Not unless they talk."

He and Renn watched as four androids brought the two expelled Eli back inside alive and encased in an air bubble or. "Ingenious idea, Commander. I wouldn't have thought of it."

"Even I could tell that Paul was ready to cave," Renn said as the two walked out of the hangar. "He just needed the right incentive. Men like him are afraid to die; thus, he cracked."

"As a synthetic life form, I have no concept of life and death."

"I think you do more than you allow yourself to. Otherwise, you would have let the baby mammoth die. Now, let's go find out what these scum balls have done to my ship."

When the two entered the interrogation room, Paul was chowing down on plates of food with a content smile.

"Talk," Renn said. "What have you done to my station?"

"Just a few more bites," Paul said as he reached for another sandwich.

Using his right arm, Renn shoved all the food off the table and onto the floor. "Tell me, or I'll shove you out of that airlock myself. Who are your companions?"

"Okay, okay," Paul stuttered. "Don't go getting your underwear in a wad. I'll tell you what I know. They belong to an alien race that deals in contraband trading. They call themselves the Ellie, the Ulli."

"The Eli?"

"Yeah, that's it. The day after you and Glogg addressed the United Nations, they approached me and asked if I would mind helping them. In return, I was guaranteed a ticket off the planet and lots of money to start over somewhere."

"What did they tell you they wanted?"

"Just a few of your animals that are stored here. You have so many, and I didn't see the harm in helping them. Plus, I wanted to be off that planet. Like you said, even if the ISC sent another watch station, the planet was dead already. It was also a chance to get rid of my crazy ex-wife."

"How did you get aboard?"

"Somehow, they knew where you would pick up the group of newcomers. We just went to the location and slipped aboard when no one was watching. To cover up our arrival, someone changed the records. We mingled in with the rest."

"No one knew of the emergency transports," Renn said. "Glogg didn't decide until a few hours before we left."

"Someone with high access had to pass that information down to Cornelius from the station," Xavier said. "Someone who also has access to the station's computer and could alter the logs. We thought it might have been Master Kim who doctored the logs, but he wouldn't have known about the transports. "He was not informed of the newcomers until a day or so after they stepped onto the hangar floor."

"Could there be more than one saboteur on board?" Renn asked."

"Possibly." Xavier turned back to Paul, who had sheepishly grabbed a nearby piece of donut. "Did Cornelius ever say who his contact person was?"

"No," Paul answered.

"Did he or any of you four have anything to do with the problems we are experiencing on the station?" Renn asked.

"Indirectly," Paul replied. "Cornelius needed to slow the station down to give his marauders time to reach us. He caused an opening in the outer shell, which would cause you to stop and make repairs. Since the animals in the Habitat Sphere were his main objective, Cornelius planned the accident to occur close to the sphere. He hoped that the space station would become unstable and that it would force you to eject the sphere. But something went wrong, and the breach happened on the other end of the station."

"Did he say why that happened?"

"Something to do with tilithium."

"What about tilithium?"

"He mentioned that the wall outside the Habitat Sphere was reinforced with tilithium and that, in some circumstances, it could become unstable. He injected some liquid into the wall to cause the tilithium to disband and break apart."

"Do you know what he used?" Renn asked again.

"No. But Cornelius said that whatever he used had spread throughout the ship and caused the first rupture."

"Did you cause the tanks in the Habitat Sphere to dysfunction?"

"We were going to. When you pulled the sphere back inside, Cornelius realized he needed a disaster to make you abandon it. But he never had time to do it."

"Why not?"

"It happened on its own."

"None of you had anything to do with the failures in the Habitat Sphere?"

"Nope." Paul eyed a piece of pie teetering on the edge of the table. "Can I have that piece of pie?"

"After you tell us the rest."

"That's all I know. Cornelius was working on a scheme to get you to eject the Habitat Sphere."

Renn reached over, grabbed the piece of pie, and slid it over to Paul.

"If you think of anything else, let the guard know."

"Will do," Paul said, stuffing the pie into his mouth. As Renn and Xavier were walking through the door, they heard Paul say. "Oh, Commander. I just remembered something. I heard Cornelius tell the other two that this station was a ticking time bomb, that the tilithium would soon tear this ship apart."

"Thanks, Paul. Enjoy your pie."

"We have to tell him," Xavier said, his voice tight with urgency. The clang of metal echoed through the cramped control room as another tremor rattled the station.

"I'm not sure now's the time," Glogg mumbled, his gaze flickering between the flashing console and Xavier's determined face.

"Glogg, this station is coming apart at the seams," Xavier pressed, his voice rising slightly. "Renn is fulfilling his duty tenfold. He's practically living in that engineering bay, working around the clock to get Jenny stable. We can't withhold information any longer. It's his call, his decision."

"But no one has ever prematurely terminated a test before its completion."

"The potential implications are a station graveyard and dead crewmates, Glogg!" Xavier slammed his fist on the console, the impact barely registering over the station's groaning. "Tell him, Glogg, or I will. He has a right to know the truth, even if it breaks him."

A beep from his pocket drew Renn's attention. It was Professor Williams on the communicator display. "Professor, I hope you're not calling me with more bad news."

"No, Sir." He heard her laugh. Her voice had a friendly tone. "I was calling to ask you for a favor."

"If I can."

"Mr. Reau is a real hero over in my department. We could have lost countless species if he hadn't noticed those free-swimming fish. The staff is giving him a surprise hero party, and I'd like to present him with a letter of accommodation. It would mean a lot to him if you signed it. He thinks so highly of you."

"Sure, have someone deliver it to the bridge tomorrow, and I'll sign it."

"I was hoping to get it signed tonight since the party is tomorrow at 0-ten hundred. Would you mind if I stopped by the bridge for you to sign it, say, in an hour?"

"I'm just on my way home," Renn replied. "Why don't you stop by my apartment? I can sign it there, and you can give me a personal update on the baby mammoth, your department, and our mutual hero, Ronald."

"Oh, Sir, I wouldn't want to impose."

"It's no imposition. It would be nice to have someone to talk to."

"Do you like chili?"

"Excuse me?"

"Are you a fan of chili?"

"Yes."

"I make a mean vegan chili. I have a fresh pot simmering on my stove. I'll run by my apartment, pick it up, and bring it. See you in an hour." Before Renn could object, she terminated the call. It was chili for dinner. He quickly texted Sarina, advising her she did not need to fix him anything to eat that evening.

At exactly sixty-three minutes later, Professor Williams knocked on Renn's door.

"Three minutes late, Professor," Renn teased. "I hope this is not how you run your department."

She laughed. "Sorry. A little hamster was running around in the lift. We had to catch him before I could use it."

"Are animals still getting loose? I can't have critters running around my station chewing on the wires and circuits. This station is experiencing enough problems without that."

"A few are still getting free, but none have escaped the confinements of the Habitat Sphere. We make sure of that. That's why I couldn't leave. We couldn't chance him getting lost on another floor. Where is the dining area?"

"This way." Renn outstretched his hand, indicating the way as he walked beside her. Once more, her sheer beauty awed him, and he almost tripped over the footstool. He noticed she wore a lilac jumpsuit with little daisies on the collar. It accentuated her bosom and showed off her tiny waist. Jenny had a suit just like that. It was his favorite. How he wished he could see her in it again."

Professor Williams placed the warm chili on the dining room table. "Where are the bowls, glassware, and utensils?"

"In the kitchen."

"And where is that?" She giggled. So like his Jenny – full of life.

"I'm sorry. I'll get them." He hurried into the kitchen and grabbed the items.

"No glassware?"

"Oh, yes. Forgive me. I'm not used to entertaining. I mean, having company for dinner. Usually, one of the AIs or my daughter does this part. What would you like to drink?"

"Water would be fine. And perhaps some bread and butter to go along with the chili?"

"I think I have some of that around here."

"You know, Commander, you don't have to worry about my animals roaming your station," Professor Williams announced as she scooped chili into the two bowls. "We have erected an invisible fencing around the entire unit to keep everyone contained."

"If I'm not mistaken, three chickens and a pig got through that fence and caused plenty of problems."

"Oh, yes, Ron's fiasco with the chickens. He told me. But we've fixed the problem, and all are confident it will hold."

Renn placed a glass of water at each of their settings. Standing behind the professor, he scooted her chair in as she sat. "Aren't you the gentleman, Commander?"

"I try to be. And you can call me Renn. This isn't a formal meeting."

"You should call me Penny." Laughing, she lightly touched his arm. "My real name's Penelope, but everyone calls me Penny for short."

"Penny, it is."

"Oh, before we get gabbing and I forget, here's that letter I need for you to sign." She reached into her satchel and withdrew the letter of accommodation.

"Very nice," Renn said after reading it. He signed his name. "I am glad to see someone is giving Ronald the credit he deserves. How's he doing?"

"He can be a handful at times, but he's a great asset to the program."

Renn and Penny ate and laughed over Penny's stories about Ronald and the baby mammoth for the next two hours. She also told funny stories about Mary. Renn couldn't remember the last time he had such a delightful evening—not since his Jenny fell ill. A sorrowful look covered Renn's face as his head turned towards the bedroom. Suddenly, guilt flooded his body for enjoying another woman's company.

Noting the Commander's despair, Penny asked, "How is she doing?"

"She sleeps. Every day, I hope, will be the day she wakes up."

"What does Master Kim say?"

Renn turned, a confused look on his face. "Master Kim? What does Master Kim have to do with my Jenny?"

"Nothing, I suppose. I just figured that since he was the great-great-grandson of her maker, he might know something."

"Dr. Chi made Jenny."

Seeing she had inadvertently said something she shouldn't have, he gathered up the dishes. "I'd best go. It's getting late."

Renn grabbed her wrist so hard that she dropped the bowls on the floor, breaking each into pieces.

"Tell me what you know."

I stumbled upon an old freezer unit hidden behind our storage room. When I inquired about its non-usage, they told me that Xavier had given orders for it to be off-limits to all personnel. I knew Xavier wouldn't tell me why, so I did some investigating. I discovered an entry by Master Tii in an old journal. He had created a new, one-of-a-kind synthetic female life form that was being stored until needed. It was not to be opened until circumstances were such that she was required.

"What circumstances?"

"Renn, you're hurting me."

The commander looked down and realized how tightly he had gripped her arm. Already, it was turning blue. He released her wrist.

"It didn't say. Upon further investigation, I discovered that someone had opened the locker a little over twelve years ago. I assume it was Jenny."

"Did it mention the date the android was brought online?"

"February 12."

Renn knew that date. It was burned into his memory because it was the day his real Jenny died. Had she been activated just for him? Why? More android secrets. But not this time.

Renn forced a smile on his face. "It's not my Jenny. She was not activated until July third. I hope I didn't hurt you. I'm just very protective of Jenny."

"I know she is essential to you," a rumpled Penny replied. She bent down to pick up the broken pieces.

"I'll get those. Thank you for the delicious dinner and laughs. We'll have to do it again sometime, after Jenny wakes. The three of us can have dinner."

"Sounds good." Penny wasn't sure that would ever happen. "If you're free tomorrow, stop by and have a piece of Ron's cake."

"Will do. Good night."

"Good night, Commander." Renn held his breath as he waited for the door to close. The moment it did, he screamed into his comm link, "Xavier, get your frigging metal ass to my apartment immediately!"

Chapter 13: SECRETS FINALLY REVEALED

It usually would take Xavier fifteen to twenty minutes to arrive at the commander's door. Renn didn't notice the android arrived in only five with Glogg. When Xavier stepped through the doorway, Renn struck him with a dining room chair as hard as possible. The chair shattered, knocking Xavier down to a knee. The skin on his right temple indented ever so slightly, then returned to normal.

Glogg rushed forward and prevented Renn from picking up a second chair. "Stop, Renn. What is the matter with you?"

Renn pushed Glogg aside. "Get up, you son-of-a-bitch. Get up and fight me."

"Commander, you know you can't hurt me." A trickle of purple blood dripped from Xavier's temple.

"Looks like you're not completely invincible. Like you, I learn. I might not be able to injure you with my fist, but I sure can with the furniture."

"It is good you are learning," Xavier said as he rose, wiping the blood from his face. "How many times have you broken your hand hitting me in the jaw? Two? Three?"

"Three. But you notice I didn't use my fist this time." Faster than Xavier or Glogg expected, Renn grabbed a nearby end table and swung it over his head to crash on the android. Xavier reached out and stopped the table with one arm while grabbing the human around the neck with his other. He lifted Renn off the ground, holding his throat closed, cutting off his air supply.

"Stop it, Xavier, you're killing him," Glogg shouted as he now tried to pry Xavier's fingers away from Renn's throat.

Xavier gave no reaction. Glogg continued to claw at the android's grip, but the former commander could not release the android's death grip, even with his alien strength. Renn stopped struggling. His body turned bluish-gray and went limp. Xavier finally released his hold and dropped the almost-dead human onto the floor. Renn gasped for breath, sucking air into his lungs. He coughed as the sensation returned to his neck.

"I WILL kill you, you son-of-a-bitch."

"Not today," Xavier replied. He walked over to the cabinet in the den, removed a glass, poured it half full of scotch, and returned to his commander. He extended it to the human. "Drink this." Renn knocked it away. Drink it, or I will pour it down your throat."

"You can try," Renn sneered.

"You doubt me?" Xavier took two steps toward the human. Renn chugged the drink, knowing Xavier would force his mouth open and pour the liquid down his throat.

"Are you happy now?"

"Not yet." Xavier watched Renn's expression intently. Xavier waited until the commander's eyes blurred and his cheeks reddened. Renn was calmer and perhaps now rational. "But perhaps if you tell me why you are trying to kill me today, I can be."

"Jenny. You lied about Jenny."

"In what way?"

"She wasn't created for me. You lied. She was crafted hundreds of years before I was even born. Master Tii made her."

"I don't know how you found out, but it is true." Xavier held out his hand. "Come, my friend, we have much to discuss."

Renn stared at the outstretched hand and hit it aside. "Go to hell."

Xavier re-extended his hand. "If you wish me to tell you the truth, come have a seat." Renn grabbed Xavier's hand, and Xavier pulled him to a stance." He slowly entered the den. He coughed, trying to ease the pain in his neck muscles.

Glogg retrieved a glass of water from the kitchen and handed it to the injured commander. "Here, I think this will help."

"You can go to hell too," Renn said, the words stinging his vocal cords. Renn turned his attention to Xavier. "I'm listening."

"I told you the truth when I said I was the last robot Master Tii ever built. But I didn't tell you that before me, he built another – my sister."

"Your sister? Jenny's your sister?"

"Yes, but I didn't know of her existence for many years. Master Tii told me of her on his deathbed. He said she was being kept in sleep in a special unit and that she was not to be awakened until it was time. When I asked him what time that would be, he said I alone would know when. He said that each of us was created for a special purpose, and again, he did not specify what. Master Tii had the gift of foresight. He witnessed something in the future that we would need to correct to ensure the continuance of life. He left each of us a little white book with secrets only we could know."

"That's what Jenny was looking for. Her book."

"Yes."

"This doesn't make sense." Renn coughed and took another sip of water. "If she was created for some particular purpose, why was she activated and given Jenny's memories?

"When you learned that the real Jenny had died, you experienced such sorrow, such remorse. I could not stand by and watch my dearest friend suffer. I thought my sister might be the answer to your salvation, so I convinced Master Kim to awaken my sister and place the real Jenny's memories in her positronic brain."

"But Doctor Chi transferred Jenny's memories."

"That's what Master Kim and I made you believe. Before we brought my sister's body to Dr. Chi, Master Kim had already done the transfer. Dr. Chi basically did nothing except run wires between the two bodies and flip a switch."

"So that's why he could never repeat the procedure. He never actually did it." Renn looked at Glogg. "Did you know this?"

"No, this is the first I've heard of this."

"Does Jenny know who or what she is?" Renn asked.

"No. I believe Jenny perceives a connection to me but does not know why. She does not know Master Tii created her or her purpose."

"But she has the white book he made for her."

"No, Jenny never had access to the book and no knowledge of it. If she now remembers it, something inside her is waking. And I don't know why." Xavier stood and walked over to a picture of Earth hanging on the wall. "But there is more, My Friend. If you want to hate me, have me disassembled, so be it. Just don't hit me over the head again."

"That depends on what you tell me?" Renn asked, his anger rising again.

"Jenny sleeps because of me. I placed her in that comma."

Xavier did not hear Renn approach until his body was yanked around to face Renn. The android expected another hit, but none came. Instead, he saw a friend devastated by Xavier's actions. "Why would you do that?"

Xavier collapsed in a nearby chair, something both Glogg and Renn never thought they'd see. "Because I didn't know what else to do. When I opened her up that day, I noted the reddish-brown tilithium infection trying to take over her body, an infection I could not save her from. I realized her dilemma was my fault. I never should have activated her. You were not her purpose. I jeopardized her mission and purpose because of my desire to end your suffering."

"But why would my suffering bother you?"

"Because it was something I could never attain. Your love for the real Jenny was so pure and inspiring that I wanted it to continue - for both of us."

"I never knew of your desire to love." Renn turned to Glogg. "Did you?"

"No, I had no idea."

"Well, you both know now. I failed Jenny. I failed you. I failed Master Tii. But most of all, I failed myself. I allowed personal desires to cloud my judgment. I should be terminated."

"We will discuss that option later." Renn softly placed his hand on the big android's shoulder. Never had he seen Xavier so vulnerable. "Can you awaken her?"

"No. I've tried."

"What about Master Kim? Can he?"

"No. He tried, but he was also unsuccessful. I put Jenny in her sleep, but she keeps herself there." Xavier looked into Renn's eyes. "I hope she is fighting the virus that is spreading inside her. When and if she does, she will awaken. Not before."

"Do you think she can defeat it?" Glogg asked.

"I do not know," Xavier replied. "If she were any other android, I would say there was no chance. But she is special, like me. Master Tii may have foreseen this and placed inside her the means to survive."

"Thank you for telling me your secrets," Renn said, touching the dried blood on Xavier's face. "I hope I didn't do too much damage."

"Nothing that can't be repaired."

"Well, gentlemen, I will not say this was a good evening, but I need time to decipher all this information alone."

"Renn, there is more."

"More? What more could there possibly be?"

Xavier positioned himself on the other side of the table, away from any furniture Renn might throw at him. "Would you mind sitting, Renn? What we're about to tell you, you're really not going to like. All I ask is that you listen and let us explain." Xavier looked over at Glogg. "Tell him."

Glogg sat in silence, his face like stone.

"TELL HIM."

"Tell me what?" Renn gave Glogg a glaring stare.

"Renn, you were so distraught when we arrived you didn't notice Xavier entered only minutes after your call," Glogg said. "That's because he was next door with me. We were getting ready to come and talk to you."

"About what?"

Glogg sighed deeply. "We've known about Cornelius and his three followers since they arrived on the ship."

"What? You've known and never said a word? Either of you?"

"You were second-in-command then and didn't need to know.
I needed you to be objective to determine what they were up to. Xavier wanted me to inform you, but I said no."

"The logs. It was you who altered the logs."

"Yes," Glogg replied. "I had to ensure you didn't know the truth about them too soon. When the breaches occurred, I knew I had been wrong in hiding this from you. I planned to tell you the day I went to my quarters, but everything went to hell before I could. I got injured, and you became Head Commander. And a whole new set of protocols came into place."

"What protocols?"

"Every Head Commander is given a test to assess their worthiness of commanding the space station. I was given one, my predecessors were given them, and you will give your successor one. It is the way we have done things for millennia."

"What kind of test?"

"We had to determine if you could save this station no matter the cost. A Head Commander's duty is to the inhabitants of this space station, not his family. Were you capable of fulfilling that duty? Your love for Jenny is so strong that I had to know if it would impede your decisions. So, we fed you certain information so you could conduct your investigation but omitted certain facts. You needed to find the culprits no matter who they were and make Cornelius reveal his hand."

"You piece of crap," Renn yelled as he approached Glogg. "You know I would never let my love for Jenny or my family stop me from doing my duty." The ten-foot-tall alien clinched his body, preparing for the punch he knew was forthcoming. To Glogg's surprise, a blow did not come. When Glogg opened his eyes, Renn stood before him, his face red, staring into the alien's eyes. "You nearly got Jenny killed. If I had known about Cornelius, I would never have let her go to Mary."

"I know. I never meant for Jenny to get hurt."

"What other information don't I know?"

"We know for sure that Dr. Chi is working with Cornelius."

"And what about Juaquin? Is he involved in this, too?"

"Juaquin was working with Dr. Chi, but only under my supervision," Xavier said. "He was trying to get the doctor to reveal who his accomplices were. When he almost blew our cover, I had to shut him down and make it look like he was infected with the virus."

"So, he's not a traitor?"

"No."

"And who altered the logs on your door's construction, Glogg? Did you?"

"Yes."

"Did Dr. Chi manufacture this substance that's attacking my ship?"

"No, we believe Cornelius brought it aboard," Xavier answered.

"And this is what also is attacking my Jenny?" Renn asked.

"Yes," Glogg said.

"How dare you not tell me this information until now," Renn screamed in Glogg's face. "How can you justify betraying me like this? Is your stupid little test worth the lives of Jenny and everyone on this ship?"

"It is the way new commanders have been evaluated. I was required to test you." Glogg composed himself and sat up straight. "I do not apologize for doing my duty."

"Get out of my sight, Glogg. I never want to see your face again as long as I live. Xavier, unfortunately, I need to see your ugly face. I want you to go with me somewhere. After we save this station, you will be stripped of your rank."

"Might I ask where we're going?"

"To get some answers from Cornelius."

———————

"Commander, what are you going to do?" Cornelius snickered. "Pretend to kill me again?"

"This time, it won't be fake," Renn said.

"Your threat of death didn't scare me when I thought it was real. What makes you think now will be any different?"

"We've got a little helper." Xavier held up a syringe.

"What's that? Sodium Pentothal. Truth serum?" Cornelius laughed. "It won't work on me."

"You'll wish that is what it is," Xavier replied.

"Bring on your worst. Your time is short. And nothing you can do will make me tell you anything. Besides, you're too civilized to resort to torture. I have nothing to worry about."

Renn wanted to beat Cornelius' smirk right off his face. He needed answers. The lives of every living creature in the space station were in danger. Renn would never resort to torture, but what else could he do?

"You're right, Mr. Waterford. I am too civilized to sink as low as you and use torture to obtain the information I want. As I mentioned to you before, my counterpart does not suffer from that affliction." Renn looked at his watch - 0-nine hundred and forty-six. "There is a piece of cake waiting for me at the celebration of a young hero. Xavier, let me know when he talks."

As he left the room, he heard Cornelius yell. "Your heap of metal is wasting his time, too."

Renn knew Cornelius would not hold that belief for long. The syringe Xavier held contained Bentigon fire-fly venom. Just two drops would burn a man from the inside out. But diluted, it also had the property to make one tell the truth. And that's what he needed—the facts. With no remorse, Xavier would use the dosage required to get the truth. That was the one aspect of the police soldiers Renn disagreed with, even if it was sometimes necessary.

As Renn stepped out of the lift onto the Habitat Sphere floor, he witnessed the celebration in Ron's honor. The room resounded with happy sounds and songs. But he could not shake the remembrance that the halls around the holding room would now be filled with the screams of their three prisoners. "God, forgive me."

Renn's thoughts were disrupted when Professor Williams walked towards him with a piece of yellow cake with chocolate frosting. He noticed the arm he had grabbed the previous night was in a sling. Had he been so mad, so ruthless, that he broke her arm?

"Commander, you made it," she greeted. "Ron will be so pleased."

He took the cake, never taking his eyes off her arm. "Professor, did I do that? Did I break your arm?"

"Oh, no, no," she replied with a smile. "It's just a little sore. A little bruised. Keeping it in a sling is easier so people don't bump into it."

"May I see it?"

"Oh, I don't think there's any need for that," the Professor nervously said. "Let's go see our guest of honor."

"Professor Williams, I want to see your arm." Renn's voice was authoritative and commanding. Placing the cake on a nearby table, he gently grabbed her arm and removed it from the sling around her neck. The skin visible beneath the large gauze wrap was a greenish blue. Carefully, he unwound the bandage and gasped at the sight of her wrist. The skin was a deep purplish-black color with thumbprints of black visible. The tissues were swollen. "Professor, I am so sorry. I never meant to hurt you like this." Renn looked at her with tears in his eyes. He had never hurt a woman before in his life, either intentionally or unintentionally.

"It's okay, Commander," Penny replied, wiping her tears. "I know you didn't mean to do it. I should never have told you what I did. I thought you knew."

"That is no excuse." Renn carefully rewound the gauze and placed her arm back in the sling. "I see Ronald is rather busy over there with his admirers. Tell him I stopped by. I must take care of some business."

"Renn, you don't need to go," Penny whispered. "Don't worry about what happened. I know you would never intentionally hurt me or anyone."

Oh, how wrong she was. In just the past twenty-four hours, Renn had smashed a chair over Xavier's head, almost pulverized the wounded Glogg, nearly broken her arm, and was currently allowing Xavier to torture three prisoners.

Without so much as a bite of cake, he turned and left. He started for the bridge but didn't think he could sit still for long. There was only one place he wanted to be, and that was with his Jenny.

Renn entered his apartment and went immediately into the bedroom. Tears filled his eyes as he watched the unconscious AI, his precious Jenny. Renn pulled up a chair beside Jenny and sat.

"Oh, Sweetheart, I miss you so much. I need you now more than ever. You see, I haven't been doing very well lately. Professor Williams stopped by last night. You remember her, don't you? Red hair, in charge of the Habitat sphere? Anyway, she told me a secret about you, and I went ballistic. I almost broke her arm. Oh, Jenny, you should see it. It's all bruised and swollen. After she left, I tried to kill Xavier. I know I've tried that before, but this time, I caused him to bleed. Can you imagine? He actually bled. I know, I know, I must learn to control my temper. That's why I need you here, to remind me. After attacking Xavier, I almost attacked Glogg and told him I never wanted to see him again." Renn stood and paced before the bed. "And worst of all, right this minute, I've allowed Xavier to torture, yes, torture, three prisoners." He stopped. "Why? Because they may have the answer on how to save you. And the ship." He sat down and took her hand in his. "Jenny, can you forgive me?" His tears poured from his eyes as he cried aloud. His torment echoed throughout the apartment. For the next two hours, the tormented soul inside the Commander cried, surrendering the burden consuming him, confessing his sins, and begging his companion to awaken.

A knock on his bedroom door made him bolt upright. He had nodded off for a while. "Yes?"

"Dad, Xavier's here to see you," Sarina reported. "Your supper is in the kitchen, ready for you when you are. And a Professor Williams stopped by and brought you some cake. She said you forgot it when you left the Habitat Sphere."

"So I did," Renn said, stretching and standing. He kissed Jenny before entering the living room where his daughter and second-in-command waited.

"Do you need me to stay?" Sabrina asked. She noticed that her father's eyes were red and puffy. Had he been crying?

"No, I don't plan on going anywhere tonight," Renn said. "You go home." He kissed his daughter on the cheek and walked her to the door. Upon closing it, he turned to Xavier. "Any success?"

"I've never known the serum not to work."

"It doesn't bother you, does it, torturing other sentient beings?"

"You know, I was designed to perform such practices without remorse or regret. I am what I am. Don't dwell on it, Renn."

"But torturing is wrong for any reason."

"Yes, it is, but sometimes it is necessary, Renn. Just realize I take no pleasure in it."

"Did all three survive?"

"Why do you ask questions you don't want the answers to?"

"What did they say?"

"As Paul told us, they came to get access to the specimens in the Habitat Sphere. They have many buyers already waiting for the contents."

"What about the liquid Cornelius injected into the station's walls?"

"I found out where he had hidden a bottle of it. Master Kim is analyzing it now. Supposedly, from what Cornelius said, it's a special serum created by the Kenndo for dissecting ships."

"I've heard of them. They're salvagers. Alloy dealers, aren't they?"

"Yes, the best in the galaxy."

"But why would they create such a liquid? They aren't marauders or bandits. They're peaceful junk dealers who dispose of all that space garbage floating out there."

"True, but the liquid enables them to tear apart a full-sized spacecraft in days instead of months. It increased their production rate fifty-fold. Its intended purpose was never for piracy or illegal activities. Once we have communications, we must report this to the ISC so they can outlaw its production.

"I agree. Is there more of this stuff on my station, or did you get it all?"

"The supply I found was minimal," Xavier replied. "I believe he has more hidden somewhere aboard the vessel, but I could not acquire that information."

Renn was curious about whether his Security Officer could not obtain the information because he had set limits on how much he would torture someone or if he had killed the prisoner. He never wanted to know which of the two possibilities was true.

"Now that we have a sample of the liquid, I have the computer searching the entire ship for a larger supply hidden somewhere on the station."

"Did he say anything about our visitors that keep popping up on our radar screens?"

"At first, he was reluctant to discuss the matter, but finally confessed an Eli fleet of a hundred fighters would arrive at our coordinates in three days."

"Three days?"

"Yes, but he also stated the ship wouldn't last that long?"

"What does that mean?"

"He said the tilithium used in the station's construction became unstable because of all the space folding we've done. The introduction of the Kenndo liquid caused a chain reaction, destroying the bonds between the carbon and nitrogen atoms. It has grown exponentially, and now all tilithium used in the ship is affected."

"What about the androids that have tilithium?"

"Unknown. Master Kim is trying to determine that."

"Can we neutralize it?"

"No. It's like a cancer eating away at the alloy bonds. No known substance can stop it."

Suddenly, the floor beneath Renn and Xavier shook, almost knocking them to their knees.

"What in the hell was that?" Renn asked.

"I'm getting reports from all over the station. Ceilings are collapsing, floors are opening up, and walls are crumbling."

"And the outer walls? Any new openings?"

"No, the force field is holding her together – for the moment."

"I thought we had three days."

"It would seem Mr. Waterford was misinformed or lied to me."

"Give the evacuation alarm," Renn ordered. "Launch the Habitat Sphere and Habitat Biospheres."

"Aye, Sir."

"Commander Oglich, I need the Command Ship and the two destroyers in the hangar now to evacuate as many life forms and androids as possible. Stop all forward movement. The station is coming apart."

"We can see that from out here. It will take at least seventy minutes to get the ships inside."

"We don't have seventy minutes."

"Have the pilots launch the remaining flies in the bay. They can carry passengers to the Command Ship as we try to bring her in."

"Make it so." Renn punched in new numbers. "Steven, I need you to get Jenny and take her, Sabrina, Jeremy, and Timmy to the hangar right away. Get them on a transport to the Command Ship."

"Renn, what's happening? What about Mary?"

"Mary is evacuating in the Habitat Sphere biosphere. This ship is coming apart. You have little time. Go."

"Sir, security reports that the ceiling above the holding room collapsed, killing one of them. Cornelius escaped."

"What about the other guy?" Xavier just shook his head. Renn didn't want to know if he had died in the interrogation or just now. "Notify security to keep a lookout for Cornelius. He may try to get aboard one of the transports."

"Sir, you must go with your family when they arrive."

"Not until I find that bastard that destroyed my station," Renn angrily shouted as he grabbed a gun from inside the den. He dashed out the door with Xavier right behind him. This time, Xavier did not advise him to go slowly.

———————

Mary and Ron took Rose, the baby mammoth, outside the biosphere to a large room where she could run and play. She loved playing ball, knocking the two down, lying on top of them, and running her trunk over their heads. Mary and Ron were her adopted family, and she loved them.

Suddenly, Rose stopped and flared her ears. She raised her trunk and sniffed the air. A wave of motion sped across the floor, loosening the floorboards.

"What's happening?" Mary asked, trying to keep her balance.

"I don't know, but I think we'd best get Rose and us back to the biosphere," Ron answered as he grabbed Rose's rope. An ear-piercing alarm sounded, scaring the young animal. She raised her head, pulling her rope from Ron's hand. Terrified, the animal bolted out the door and down the hallway, away from the biosphere.

"You go back," Ron said. "I'll get Rose."

"No, I'm coming with you."

"No, it's too dangerous. Get inside the biosphere before it leaves."

"You two must get back to the biosphere right away," Glogg ordered as he suddenly appeared in the doorway with Professor Williams.

"Where's Rose?" the professor asked.

"She got spooked and ran."

"We don't have time to find her," Professor William declared. "I want you two back inside now."

"No, you take Mary. I can't leave without Rose. She's my responsibility." Before anyone could object, Ron ran after the small mammoth.

"Ron, come back here," Professor Williams shouted.

"Do as Ron suggested," Glogg yelled. "I'll get Ron and hopefully Rose, too."

"You've only got twelve minutes, Commander. After that, the door will lock and seal. And there is no way I can open it."

"Understood." Glogg fled after the young man who caused him such headaches. He would not allow him to die today.

Chapter 14: JENNY'S MESSAGE

"What about Mary?" Sarina shouted over the alarm.

"Your dad said she's leaving on the Habitat Sphere biosphere," Stephen replied, pushing his wife and sons toward the door.

The floor shook again, more violently this time. All three were knocked off their feet. The kitchen ceiling collapsed, and the front door split in two. Sarina screamed.

Getting to his feet, Steven ran to the front door. He tried to move the door, but the pieces were wedged into the frame and wouldn't budge. Looking around, Steven picked up one of the wooden chairs and smashed it into the door. The door cracked but did not give way. Seeing what his father was trying to do, Jeremy grabbed a chair and smashed it into the door. A large section broke free, large enough for the four to escape.

"Jeremy, take Timmy and your mom to the hangar," Steven ordered. "I'll get Jenny."

"Dad, she's too heavy for you to carry alone. I'm staying. Mom and Timmy should go."

Steven quickly kissed his wife goodbye. "Take Timmy. We'll be right behind you in just a few minutes."

"You'd better," Sarina replied. Grabbing Timmy's hand, the two ran down the hallway weaving around the destruction on the floor.

When the father and son arrived at Renn's residence, they encountered a giant beam blocking the door. Behind the barrier, the door was dislodged as theirs had been.

"Dad, how are we going to get Jenny?"

"I don't know. Even if we can move this beam out of the way, Renn's door is fortified. There'll be no breaking or budging it."

"We can't leave her in there. Grandfather would never forgive us. He's counting on us."

"I know, I know," Steven said, rubbing his head as he walked in a tight circle, trying to determine what to do.

———————

"Rose, where are you?" Ron yelled as he stopped at a six-way intersection. He had no idea which way the little mammoth ran. He heard Rose trumpet in fear and followed the sound down a short corridor. Upon turning a corner, he saw Rose in a conference room. Cornelius had a rope around her neck and was dragging her towards a flier waiting outside the force shield.

"Where are you taking Rose?" Ron shouted as he rushed forward. A large section of the floor between Ron and Cornelius collapsed, creating an impassable cavern.

"She'll fetch a pretty price on the market," Cornelius snickered. "At least I'll get something in compensation for all my troubles."

"No, I won't let you take her." Ron calculated the distance across the chasm. If he got up enough speed, he might make it. He ran back ten feet, then turned. Summoning all his energy, he ran forward, preparing to leap across the gaping expanse. Cornelius fired at Ron. The blast hit the flooring beneath Ron's feet, causing the floor section to give way. Screaming, Ron plummeted into an eight-floor-deep chasm.

"Ronald," Glogg shouted as he watched the young hero disappear. Glogg lifted his gun and fired, hitting Cornelius in the shoulder. Dropping the rope, the perpetrator ran off down the hall. Instinctively, Glogg jumped into the chasm.

Seeing they had missed their chance, the Eli ship outside prepared to leave. But three ISC fliers blocked his way. Help had finally arrived.

———————

Renn and Xavier ran through the station, searching for Cornelius. Substantial debris caused by the failing vessel impeded their path. The ship moaned as it strained against its bulkheads.

"She's not going to stay together much longer," Renn shouted.

"With this much of her on the floor, I'm surprised she's held this long," Xavier shouted back as he crawled under hanging cables. Xavier listened to his internal communications and smiled. "We've got him. He's heading for the small hangar bay on deck twenty-seven. And I have several reports that the ISC has arrived and is helping to evacuate our inhabitants."

"About bloody time," Renn shouted in glee.

They paused for a moment in the hallway before the hangar door. Xavier knew Renn needed to catch his breath. He quickly scanned the commander and noted his heart rate was too high but within acceptable bounds.

"Ready to get the Cutuff?" Renn asked.

Xavier looked at Renn in surprise. "Sir, such language is inappropriate for a Head Commander, even if Cornelius is one."

The sound of running footsteps silenced the two. They waited with guns drawn, hoping it was their culprit. Within seconds, a scared

Cornelius came around the corner. Renn fired and missed. Xavier did not, clipping Cornelius' leg. Cornelius stumbled and landed eight yards in front of them. On his way down, Cornelius fired on Xavier. A cold sensation spread across the android's body as a pulsating energy compromised his systems. He fell hard onto the floor, able to see everything but unable to move.

"No, this isn't possible. I am indestructible."

"Surprising what some good Keeno serum can do," Cornelius shouted.

Distracted by the invincible android's fall, Renn paused for a moment. It was what Cornelius was waiting for. He fired, shooting Renn in the upper thigh. As Renn spun around, he fired blindly, shouting the gun out of Cornelius' hand. Cornelius leapt up with a knife in his uninjured hand and charged the Commander, knocking him to the floor. Renn grabbed Cornelius' hand, trying to keep him from plunging the knife's blade deep into his chest. But Renn was weak from running. The knife grew closer to his heart with each heartbeat.

Xavier watched in horror, unable to move. "Jenny, Renn needs you," he shouted inside his core.

———————

In the Head Commander's bedroom, the room shook violently as pieces of ceiling tower and plaster rained down, jolting the once peaceful space into chaos. Jenny was abruptly awakened by the havoc. Her eyes flew open, wide with fear and confusion, as she quickly assessed the situation. Dust filled the air, making it hard to see, and the sound of crumbling plaster echoed around her. Her heart pounded in her chest as she heard Xavier's desperate message.

Amid the disarray, a single name escaped her lips, filled with a mix of urgency and concern, "Renn." Her voice was barely a whisper, yet it cut through the noise. She instinctively reached out, searching for any sign of him, her thoughts racing. She accessed her memories of the past few days and pieced together what caused her fear.

"I'm coming, Renn," Jenny shouted as she jumped to her feet.

They tried as they could, but Jeremy and Steven could not get the front door to move even an inch. Knowing that time was short, they tried one last time to no avail.

"Dad, do you hear something?" Jeremy asked, pressing his ear against the door.

"It sounds like someone's in there."

To their surprise, the door was pulled open. Jenny stood there, the door in her left hand.

"Jenny."

"Grandma."

"Get to the transport."

"What about you?" Jeremy asked.

"I'm going to go save your grandfather and this ship."

Xavier's weapon was just three inches from his fingertips, but he couldn't reach it. The imposter was stronger than his Commander, and it was only minutes until Renn's strength to hold the knife at bay would fail him. A blur rushed past the android and leapt into the air. As Jenny screamed, she plunged a hunter's knife into Cornelius' neck, slicing him open from his jawbone down to his tailbone.

In shock, Cornelius turned and looked at the female AI. "I thought you were dead."

"Not yet."

The sliced-open, lifeless body fell onto the floor.

"Jenny, you're okay," Renn shouted as he pulled her into his arms. "I never thought I'd see you again. How?"

"I'll let Xavier explain it to you."

"Help me up. We need to go."

"No, I must save the station. It was what I was created for."

"Jenny, you're not making sense. It is not your responsibility to save the ship."

She kissed Renn passionately. "Remember, I will always love you." She turned to Xavier. "Take care of him."

"Always."

Jenny freed herself from Renn's hold and ran towards the outside wall. It started to glow as the molecular structure of the tilithium was reaching critical status.

"Come back, Jenny. That floor is going to give way." Ren tried standing, but his thigh injury was too severe, and he crumbled back onto the floor. Ignoring the pain, he clawed at the floor, dragging himself forward inch by inch, trying to get to her before the room collapsed. If they were going to die, they'd die together in each other's arms.

"Xavier, the ship's computer has located a large supply of tilithium," Jenny shouted. "It is feeding the destruction of the ship. It's located in hangar 2-X on the lower deck. Eject it. It's too powerful for me."

"Jenny, stop," Renn pleaded, no longer caring about anything but her.

Xavier's mind connected with his sister's, enabling him to access the tilithium's location. He activated the controls in the small hangar to eject the tilithium, but the doors did not open.

"Jenny, the controls are neutralized," Xavier said. "I can't open the hangar's doors. Can you try?"

"I need all my concentration to keep the wall together. We need to find someone else to open the doors."

The beeper on his belt sounded as Jeremy waited with his family to board the spaceship. He looked down and found a message from Xavier. "Incapacitated. You must awaken Juaquin in holding room 2-B, floor 2, subsection A-D."

"How do I awaken him?" Jeremy texted.

"Push the black button in his right armpit. That will reactivate him. Once he is functional, say, 'Xavier command 1-1-code J3'. He will know what to do."

"Dad, I have to go wake Juaquin."

"Son, you can't go anywhere. We must get on the transport."

"Xavier just messaged me. He's hurt and can't do it himself. If I don't, the ship will fail."

Steven knew that trying to reach the unconscious AI was a death sentence. But he also knew Xavier would not give his son such a mission unless it were imperative. "I'll go with you." He turned to his wife. "Don't ask any questions. Just get you and Timmy on the transport. Jeremy and I have something to do." Saying no more, the two men ran towards the hangar doors.

"No one may leave," said the android guarding the door.

"I have orders from Xavier," Jeremy said.

"No one may leave," the AI repeated.

"Xavier, they won't let me leave," Jeremy texted.

"What is the robot's designation?"

Jeremy looked at the name tag on the AI unit. "Samual 4-F."

The guarding android listened briefly to the message inside his head. "The boy may proceed, but you, Mr. Spalling, must remain," the android announced.

"No, I'll not let my son go alone."

"He won't be. I am going with him."

Jeremy placed his hand on his dad's shoulder. "It will be okay, Dad. I can do this. You take care of Mom and Timmy."

"No, Jeremy. It's too dangerous."

"Sam here will protect me. Trust me. I need to go now, Dad. I don't have much time."

Steven hugged his son, knowing there was no greater protection than a security android. "I do trust you. Good luck."

"Follow me," the android said as the doors opened, and he ran through.

Jeremy ran after him. "Do you know where you are going?"

"Yes, Xavier told me. Holding room 2-B, floor 2, subsection A-D. It will help if you run faster. We have little time to complete our mission."

"I'm running as fast as I can," Jeremy said. His muscles were already straining, and the sweat was flowing from his body.

"This is not a sufficient speed." Without warning, Sam picked Jeremy up in his arms and sprinted to the elevators. They were on floor 1-B, and the room where Juaquin slumbered was above them.

A steel beam that fell from the ceiling smashed the elevator door, blocking their way. "Now, what do we do?" Jeremy asked. "How can we get to the second floor?"

Placing Jeremy on the floor, Sam quickly analyzed their situation. "There, the emergency hatch." The android walked to a wall panel, grabbed it, and threw it aside, revealing an access ladder. "We'll need to climb up. Get on my back, and I will carry you."

"I can do it myself."

"No, you are too slow. Remember?"

Knowing there was no time to argue, Jeremy did as asked. Within seconds, the android was scaling up the ladder with the human on his back. Thanks to Sam's speed, it only took two minutes to reach the second floor. After exiting the access, both ran to the holding room. This time, Sam let Jeremy run on his own power.

Upon entering the room, the two found the still body of Juaquin lying on a stretcher. Jeremy hurried over and tried to lift the android's right arm, but it was too heavy.

"Sam, I need to access Juaquin's armpit. Can you lift his arm for me?"

"Yes."

Sam grabbed Juaquin's wrist and lifted the arm with little effort. Jeremy searched and found inside the armpit a tiny black freckle. Assuming that was the correct button, Jeremy pushed it and waited. A slight humming filled his ears as Juaquin's eyes flew open.

"Juaquin, Xavier command 1-1-code J3."

Juaquin bolted into an upright position. He jumped from the stretcher, grabbed Jeremy, threw him over his shoulder, and rushed from the room.

"I hope this isn't going to be normal, you guys carrying me," Jeremy said as the two androids raced towards the small hangar.

———————

"Xavier, I can't hold it much longer," Jenny shouted, her strength slipping away with each passing second.

"Jeremy's almost there," Xavier said. "Hold on for just another few seconds. Let me try to connect with you and transfer some of my power to you." He closed his eyes and searched within his positronic brain for a way to do the impossible. He had never attempted such a feat before, but somehow, he knew a transfer to his sister was possible – another "special secret" Master Tii had given the two androids. Locating the program, Xavier pushed out from his body a bolt of energy. It flowed from his body into the floor, across the boards, up through her body, and out through her fingertips. Her energy force doubled in strength as the wall molecules reconnected.

"Jenny, take me with you," Renn pleaded as he crawled closer.

"Where is it?" Jeremy asked, running around the room, trying to find the supply of tilithium. "It has to be here somewhere."

"Our alien friends would have hidden it well. It cannot be seen with human vision." Juaquin switched to various advanced optics until, at last, he located a shimmer behind the left wall. "It's there." He and Sam ripped apart the wall revealing five large canisters of the deadly liquid.

"We've got to eject this stuff now," Juaquin said.

"But how? It's too heavy to move?" Jeremy asked.

"If we open the bay doors, everything inside this room will be sucked out, including the canisters," Juaquin said.

"And us with them," Jeremy said. "I can't breathe without air, remember."

Juaquin walked over, grabbed the only jetpack from the wall, and handed it to Sam. "You must take the human back to the transport. He cannot survive the doors being opened."

"Sir, you outrank me. It is my life that should be jeopardized, not yours. There is the possibility that whoever ejects the palate will not survive. That must be me."

Juaquin put on the jet pack, attached a lifeline to one of the bulkheads, and took Jeremy into his arms. "Do not worry, Jeremy. I will not let you die." As Juaquin gave an affirmative nod, he encased the human and himself in an airtight bubble. Sam pushed the button. The outside doors lifted, causing an enormous vacuum. Within seconds, anything on the floor or in the hangar was pulled into space except for one android and one scared human. These two beings floated in the air, suspended by their tether. Both watched a protective film cover Sam as he flew into space. Hopefully, it would keep the android's insides from freezing until help could retrieve him.

The wall beside Renn was moving away from Jenny, not towards her. He looked around and saw Xavier holding on to his uninjured leg, pulling him back. The strength in Xavier's arm muscles was returning.

"What are you doing, you fool? Let go of me."

"Today is not your day to die, Renn. It's hers."

Renn's eyes opened in terror as he comprehended what Xavier was saying. "No, she can't." He turned back around toward the love of his life. "Don't do it. Don't leave me, Jenny." Determined to move forward, Renn kicked at Xavier's hand repeatedly until the android's skin ripped open and purple blood oozed out. "Let go!" But Xavier kept a tight hold.

"I can't do that."

Ignoring the happenings behind her, Jenny stood before the crumbling corridor and outstretched her arms towards the ceiling and across the wall. Her hands glowed, and rays of bright light emerged from her fingers, shooting outward, spreading across the wall, and ceiling. A soft blue light traveled up the rays and through the station, bonding the alloy atoms together. As the bond grew stronger, the breaks in the hull sealed. The wall cracks disappeared, and the floors became solid again. Jenny was healing the broken station.

"No, Jenny," Renn shouted. "Stop, or you'll die."

She turned and smiled at him as more connections joined her to the station. "This is my purpose, the reason Master Tii created me. I, and I alone, have what is needed to stop this catastrophe."

"No, it's not. Why do you say that?"

"I love you."

A hum started and grew in intensity as the walls vibrated. Renn covered his ears to deafen the sound. A blinding flash filled the room, making both human and artificial life forms close their eyes. When they opened them, the glow was gone. The danger was neutralized, and the destruction of the ship halted. Jenny lay motionless on the floor.

Knowing the end had come for his sister, Xavier let go of Renn's leg. Adrenalin pumping through his body, Renn lifted himself onto his good leg and hobbled forward. Ignoring the pain that coursed through his body, Renn dragged his injured leg across the floor. A wide trail of deep red blood trailed behind him across the floor. When he reached Jenny's side, he dropped to the floor, screaming in pain. Renn reached out and pulled Jenny into his arms, cradling her on his chest. "I'm here, Jenny. Talk to me. Don't go, Jenny, unless you take me with you."

Jenny slowly opened her eyes, but their luster was gone. Her skin was clammy and cold. She reached up and wiped the tears from Renn's cheek. "Today is not your day to die, Renn. You must stay and watch over our family." Renn sobbed uncontrollably. "Do not cry, My Love. This is the way it must be. This is why Master Tii made me."

"No, you can't leave me. I won't let you."

"You can't stop the inevitable." Jenny's breathing slowed as she stared into space as if her eyes had ceased functioning. Her body was shutting down. "Kiss me goodbye."

Renn lifted her closer to his face, leaned down, and softly pressed his lips to hers. He felt their contact, but the life within her soon disappeared.

"No, Jenny, don't leave me. Please. Come back. Come back." He rocked back and forth with his soulmate in his arms, pressing her close to his heart. He could not speak because of the magnitude of his tears. His body shook in waves of despair as he screamed in sorrow.

Beneath Xavier, a pool of tears formed on the floor. His emotions expanded and engulfed him as he experienced the loss of his sister.

———————

"Any change?" Xavier walked up to Steven, Sarina, Glogg, and Dr. Robinson, who waited around the corner of the hallway from where Jenny had died. Fresh gun marks on the walls indicated Renn was still firing at anyone who approached.

"It's been three days," Sarina said, wiping the tears from her eyes. "He won't let anyone near her. He keeps repeating for her to come back."

"He's in pretty bad physical shape," Dr. Robinson stated. "We must do something now. He'll never survive another day. He's dehydrated, lost a lot of blood, and that thigh wound needs attending."

"Unfortunately, that damn gun he possesses has an unending supply of rounds," Steven said. "He'll die before he runs out of ammo."

"So, what's the plan?" Xavier asked.

"I have one of Professor Williams' animal tranquilizer guns," Dr. Robinson answered. "Sarina and Steven will keep him distracted while I sneak around the side and shoot him. Once he's out, I can get him to sick bay and hopefully save his life."

"Even in his delirious state, he's too much of a trained soldier to fall for that trick," Xavier said. "I have something I'd like to try."

"Xavier, he hasn't listened to you the other times you tried," Sarina said. "You've already taken a bullet twice. Why do you think this time will be different?"

"I just do. If it doesn't work, we'll use the tranquilizer gun. Have the gurney ready to transport him if I give you the signal."

Xavier walked around the corner towards the commander. Renn was sitting with his back leaning against the wall, holding Jenny in his arms. A pool of urine and blood surrounded him. His torn pant leg revealed a large wound in his upper thigh. The skin was dark and oozing a greenish slim. Renn's face was drawn and an ashy gray, his eyes sunken and surrounded by dark circles. His body was weakening, and he had trouble maintaining his hold on Jenny. She slipped two inches down his chest. Renn did not have the strength to lift her back up. Dr. Robinson was right – Renn would not survive another day. When Jenny slipped again and Renn tried to hold her, Xavier noted dark patches covering Jenny's skin. She was starting to decay.

"Hello, Dear Friend," Xavier said as he poked his head around the corner. "May I sit here?" When Renn showed no aggression, the android sat before his grieving commander.

"Go away." Came an almost inaudible voice.

"I will. But I brought something I want to read for you first."

"No." Renn strained to reach his weapon on the floor, but his muscles were too weak to accomplish the task. On the third attempt, his fingers made contact, but he could not lift it. He swung the barrel towards Xavier. "Kill you."

"What's new? You're always trying to end my existence over something." Normally, Xavier would have laughed, but not this time. Today, things were too serious, and his friend needed his help.

Watching Renn's fingers, Xavier realized the Commander didn't have to lift the weapon. He could fire it while it lay on the floor. At this close range, he might finally damage the android significantly. Perhaps even fulfill the promise of killing him.

"Go. Kill."

"Tell you what, I'm going to sit right here. I promised Jenny I would do something. After I show you, you can shoot me if you want. How's that?" Even though Renn's eyes were hazy, the look of hate was unmistakable. Xavier knew Renn blamed him for Jenny's death and for him being alive.

Xavier reached into his breast pocket and removed a small white book. He placed it on the floor so Renn could see it. "Do you know what this is?"

For just a moment, life returned to Renn's eyes. "Jenny. Book," the commander said in a hoarse voice.

"Yes, it is the book Jenny was searching for. The one with all her secrets."

"How?"

"That is one of my secrets. But, if you survive, I promise to tell you." Xavier scooted a little closer, and Renn wrapped his trigger finger around the gun. Xavier halted his advancement. "Jenny knew she was expiring, and you would have trouble dealing with her passing. Before she passed, she contacted me in that unique way androids can and asked me to explain the reason for her death. She asked me to read something to you." Xavier opened the book to a marked page. He turned the book towards Renn so he could see the writing. "Renn, is this Jenny's handwriting?"

"Yes." Came the fragile voice.

"May I read it?"

"Yes." Renn relaxed his trigger finger.

"Earth date February 27, 2051," Xavier began. "On this date, I will fulfill my purpose. Master Tii has foreseen an evil life form who will try to destroy the life the ISC has so passionately conserved. A serum that destroys the bonds of the alloy tilithium will be used to destroy the station. The possibility of it spreading across the universe is indisputable. It will end life as we know it. Master Tii has placed within me an antidote that I must use to eradicate this threat. This is my purpose. This is my ending."

Xavier stopped. Was Renn coherent enough to comprehend Jenny's words? "Renn, can you look at me?"

Renn slowly lifted his tear-swollen eyes.

"Jenny wrote this entry in her book almost five hundred years ago. The date, February 27, 2051, was three days ago, the day she passed. She knew five hundred years ago that she would die on that day. Her death is not your fault. It's not Glogg's or my fault. It's no one's. It was her destiny. Jenny knew she was the only hope to prevent a catastrophic occurrence. It was the purpose Master Tii assigned her. Does this make sense to you?"

Renn did not answer, but the android witnessed recognition in his commander's eyes. "She also asked me to give you a message. But for you to hear it, I must touch your hand. Can I do that? Can I come closer and take your hand?"

Slowly, Renn moved his hand away from the weapon and slid it across the floor towards Xavier. He did not have the strength to lift his hand off the ground. Xavier slid beside the human, slowly reached out, and took Renn's hand. "I know we've never done this before, but I am going to enter your mind so you can hear the message."

Tiny filaments emerged from Xavier's hand and entered Renn's. The android jumped as he sensed how far Renn's sorrow plummeted into his soul. Xavier never thought such loneliness, such emptiness, was possible. Like Renn's, Xavier's eyes filled with tears.

Renn drew in a deep breath when he heard Jenny's voice. "Jenny."

"My Dearest Love," Jenny's said. "I am sorry I hurt you, but I had to leave to save you, our family, the space station, and the world. And if Xavier is playing this message for you, you haven't accepted my passing or purpose. Renn, you must let me go. I fulfilled my purpose, and it is time for you to fulfill yours. Like it or not, it is not your time to die. There is much the universe has planned for you. You are the Head Commander and, as such, you must take this ship to New Earth as planned. It is you who must live. Do you hear me? You cannot die because I did. I want you to live to an incredibly old age. Find a new someone to laugh with, to talk to, to love. I know you will always love me as I love you, but you must go on. Live for both of us. And when you are ready to come home, the real Jenny and I will be waiting here for you." Her voice rose to a demand. "Now get up and go live your life." Softly, she added, "Do this for me, Renn."

"Did you hear her?" Xavier asked, barely able to speak. The sorrow from Renn's body was pouring into Xavier's and overwhelming him. He didn't know how much longer he could maintain his emotions. He wasn't used to this.

Xavier watched Renn's composure but noted no reaction. Was Renn too weak to respond? Or was he still unwilling to let Jenny's body go?

"Renn, do you remember that android skin is alive? Like yours, Jenny's skin needs air and blood to stay healthy. She's not getting that, and her skin is starting to decay. I must process her body if I want to preserve her. Don't you want her to remain and look like she always did? I have a gorgeous place ready for her where she will remain beautiful. And you can visit her every day if you'd like."

Renn looked at Jenny. Did he see she was decaying?

"Renn, please do as Jenny asked. She wanted you to live, but you are dying, my friend. You need medical attention. And soon. Let me take her and save you, save you both." Unable to contain the emotions flooding his body, tears rolled down Xavier's face. The tears turned into sobbing. "Renn, I can't lose you both. Please let me help you." Xavier waited, his sobs growing louder. "Please, Renn."

Renn squeezed Xavier's hand. Xavier looked up to see his friend staring into his eyes. "Yes. Live," came two almost inaudible words. Slowly, Renn opened his arms and allowed Jenny's body to fall. Xavier rushed forward and caught Jenny in one arm while catching Renn as he collapsed forward in the other.

"I've got you, Commander. I will always have you." Summoning his strength, Xavier shouted, "Dr. Robinson, get that stretcher in here NOW."

Chapter 15: FIFTEEN YEARS LATER

"Here she comes now," Ronald announced, pointing his finger north. He and Mary were married two years earlier and were expecting their firstborn in three days. To help celebrate the occasion, Stephen and Sarina, Jeremy with his wife and two sons, and Renn and Penny came to visit. The guests smiled as the full-grown Rose briskly walked towards them.

"Look behind Rose," Mary said. "Watch for a surprise."

From behind the pachyderm emerged a pint-sized elephant with ears that were too large and a trunk that dragged on the ground.

"Oh, she's adorable," Sarina said.

"What's this, her third calf?" Renn asked.

"No, second. Rose reached sexual maturity at ten years of age," Ron said. "Like modern elephants, their gestation period is approximately twenty-three months. They don't come back into estrous until about a year or two after the baby's birth."

"I bet you ladies are glad you don't have to carry a baby inside for two years," Jeremy teased, winking at his sister.

"I could barely do nine months, let alone two years," Mary said.

"I'm just glad Glogg saved Rose and me that day," Ron stated. "Who knew he had wings?"

"I don't think he even remembered," Renn laughed. "In all the years we worked together, he never mentioned or indicated he had those enormous wings."

"Didn't Xavier know?"

"No, or I'm sure he would have told me. We would have had some good laughs had we been aware of them," Renn added.

"When he swooped down and grabbed me after I fell into that floor break, I thought I had died, and an angel came for me," Ron said. "Imagine my surprise when I realized it was Glogg."

"Do you think he'll ever come back?" Sarina asked, watching the baby mammoth chase a flock of blackbirds.

"Doubtful," Renn answered. "With his three sons' deaths, losing his upper arm, and having almost no use of the lower arm, his heart wasn't in exploration anymore. He always wanted to take the family home to visit their homeworld. It's just over a three-hundred-year journey to Gloxin. Add another three hundred to return, and they'd be gone over six hundred years. Everyone, except for Xavier, Juaquin, and a few other AIs, would be dead and turned to dust. I think that's why he took Una, Dii, the twins, and his sister with him. He realized he'd never return."

"Did you two patch your differences before he left?" Jeremy asked.

"Yes, pretty much. I'm afraid I still disagree with what Glogg and Xavier did, but I understand they did what they were obligated to do. I can't fault either for that. But when I became Head Commander, I ensured that stupid test was stripped from the manual. No New Head Commander will ever have to be tested for their worth again."

"Have you decided on a name for the baby?" Jeremy asked Mary.

"If Grandfather has no objection, we'd like to name her Jennifer," Mary said.

Renn smiled. "Jennifer Reau. I like that. My Jenny would like that too."

"Poppie, Poppie, will you swing us?" cried his two great-grandsons as they ran towards the group and wrapped their arms around Renn's legs.

"Don't you want to watch the mammoths?" Sarina asked.

"No, we see them all the time. We want to swing."

"I'll push them, Renn," Steven announced.

"No, I will," Renn said. "Living on the station, I only get to visit them a few times a year. It would be an honor to push them."

When Renn walked away with his great-grandchildren pulling on his hands, Sarina noticed his step was a little slower. She did not witness him letting go of the littlest's hand to rub the pain in his left arm. "How's he doing? He seems to be slowing down a bit."

"He is,' Penny said. "Dr. Robinson did his six-month physical and gave him a decent bill of health last week. He has a few heart issues, and his weight is down."

"No problem with the artificial leg?" Stephen asked.

"No, not that Renn or Dr. Robinson stated. Even if it gave him problems, Renn would never complain, not when three of the bones inside belong to Jenny."

"That was a wonderful thing Xavier and Master Kim did, creating a new leg from Jenny's body for him," Sabrina said. "I think that's the only thing that got him through his loss of her - that and his friendship with you. How are you doing? Have you tried talking to him again about coming down here to live?"

"He'll never leave the station while she's up there," Penny answered. "I don't even mention the subject anymore."

"What about bringing her body down here?" Steven asked.

"I mentioned that once," Penny said. "He was against it."

"Why?"

"He didn't say."

"Does he still visit her every day?"

"Most days," Penny said. "On his way to and from the bridge, he stops by the room where she lies. He picks a daisy from the greenhouse each morning and lays it on her coffin, throwing away the previous day's flower. Sometimes, when he disappears for hours, I know he's with her."

"He visits her twice every day?"

"He's missed a few times, but they're rare. Sometimes, some pressing station problem prevents him from following his routine. He doesn't know, but sometimes I follow him. Renn tells Jenny about his day, how the family is doing, and what is happening here on New Earth. He even tells her about me and how much she'd like me."

"His visits don't bother you?" Steven asked. "I can't think of many women who would share their husband with the former wife, even if she is deceased."

"When I married Renn, I understood that Jenny would still be a major part of his life and his first love. I promised myself I would not be jealous of a ghost or an android inside a glass box. Besides, Renn is that special man capable of loving two women to his fullest in his lifetime. I do not doubt that he loves me. Maybe not as much, or in the same way he loved the real Jenny or her replica, but he always shows his love for me. I feel loved, and that's all that counts. The two Jennys may have been his first love, but I will be his last."

"Oh no," Mary shouted. "I think my water just broke."

"Renn, your great-granddaughter is coming," Sabrina shouted.

Baby Jennifer Reau was born that afternoon at 0-fifteen hundred. Renn held her in his arms and shared with her all the details about the woman she was named after. He explained the fun they were going to have together. Three days later, Commander Renn died in his sleep at one hundred and sixty-one.

Xavier asked that they place Renn's body with Jenny in the glass coffin. Penny agreed that resting with Jenny forever was the only place appropriate for the Head Commander. "A love story as wondrous as theirs should be preserved for all to remember." Sabrina agreed.

After placing Renn in his dress uniform, Xavier placed his friend inside the coffin. He placed the preserved Jenny inside Renn's arms, encircling them around her. Jenny's head rested over Renn's heart, her left arm crossing his chest and tucked under his rib cage.

Xavier's smile widened as he observed the two lying together, entwined in each other's arms. He wondered what his dearest friend would have thought if he had known how often Xavier had watched them sleep like this. Xavier was sure Renn would have been furious, considering it a betrayal of their friendship. But the viewing brought Xavier comfort. Witnessing the love between Renn, a human, and Jenny, an android, was a mirrored reflection of a life the android yearned for, a life forever out of his reach. Even now, in their quiet moments of shared death, Xavier found a strange comfort, a brush with a love he dreamt of possessing.

Upon Renn's passing, the ISC made a historic decision and promoted Xavier, making him the first artificial life form to attain the rank of Head Commander. This groundbreaking appointment came after thousands of petitions for Xavier's elevation to the esteemed position were received. When the tribunal convened to deliberate Xavier's candidacy, the chamber overflowed with citizens eager to testify on behalf of the feeling android who possessed both rational intellect and empathetic depth and had proven his exceptional capabilities on countless missions over the years. While a few dissenting voices expressed reservations about an artificial entity holding such immense responsibility, the overwhelming majority lauded Xavier's judgment and leadership. The tribunal voted to install him as Head Commander, recognizing his unique qualifications transcending biological constraints.

Xavier honored the tradition set forth by his former commander. Each day, as he traveled to and from the bridge, he detoured to the ship's greenhouse and selected a single white daisy, its petals pristine and delicate. He walked to where Renn and Jenny's coffin lay and, with reverence, placed the fresh daisy atop the coffin, removing the wilted bloom from the previous day. "Sleep well," he murmured as he ran his fingers across the smooth surface, a simple gesture conveying gratitude and respect.

Jeremy and his family spent most of their time on the planet. He was part of the military force that patrolled the sector, ensuring everyone remained free from hostile parties, and rose to the rank of Captain like his grandfather and father. In his downtime, Jeremy continued to design and build new spacecrafts with Xavier's help. Xavier admired the boy and thought highly of him.

Timmy joined the Intergalactic Air Commission. Like his older brother, he both flew and designed new ships. Unlike his siblings, Tim chose to remain single and enjoy a free life of exploration.

So that future generations would know their home planet, Earth, Sarina wrote numerous books about what the planet was like and her history. She even wrote about their journey to New Earth, telling what it was like to meet the various alien life forms for the first time and their five-year trip, including their encounter with the Eli. After Stephen retired, she took a position at the Natural History Museum, teaching a class on the blue planet for any human born after their departure.

Steven took a different route. After serving as Renn's second-in-command for ten years, he chose a simple life. He learned the art of basket weaving and became a noted artist. His baskets were sold across the galaxy and were in high demand. He was awarded several prestigious awards for his craftsmanship.

Ron and Mary had another girl and a boy. Ron never forgot the tall alien who saved his life multiple times, especially the day Glogg jumped into the cavern when the ship came apart. In his honor, he made Mary name their son Glogg.

Ron continued his promise to keep Rose safe, and with Mary's help, she lived to an old age. The couple cared for many of the animals brought on the Space station, ensuring they had good lives. For his dedication to Earth's wildlife, Ron became the first governor of New Earth.

Because Renn had shown Penny so much love, she married a biologist younger than her four years after the Commander's death. They had two children, both boys. Together, they managed the largest rainforest on New Earth.

Master Kim taught his oldest son the teachings of his great-great-great-grandfather. He explained why certain robots were unique and the story of two extra special ones. Regrettably, the two androids could never be replicated again, and the passage of centuries caused most of Master Tii's expertise to be lost.

For centuries, Xavier endured the relentless march of time, a solitary figure haunted by the loss of his dearest friend. Though the universe continued to expand and evolve, his heart remained tethered to the past, a well of sorrow that could never be filled. At last, weary of an existence devoid of Renn and Jenny's companionship, he decided to discontinue his life, entrusting the mantle of leadership to Juaquin, the next AI Head Commander.

Juaquin's first act of authority was to encase Xavier's body in an upright glass coffin, a sentinel forever frozen in time, his hand outstretched and resting atop the coffin that housed his beloved Jenny and Renn. In Xavier's hand, he held a golden metal daisy, a symbol of the enduring love and friendship that had transcended the boundaries of flesh and circuitry. He added the Spallings wing to the Museum of Natural History, a sacred space dedicated to preserving the legacy of Renn, Jenny, and Xavier. Juaquin placed the three within its halls: Xavier stood behind Jenny and Renn's glass coffin, thus maintaining his silent vigil for eternity.

Juaquin had an inscription sketched into the top portion of the glass coffin for all to read:

Here lie the true heroes of New Earth. Without their dedication and sacrifice, we would not be here. May they continue to bask in each other's friendship for all eternity.

Further below, he added:

THE END IS JUST THE BEGINNING

As word of Renn and Jenny's love spread across the galaxy, people from all corners of the universe flocked to the museum, drawn by the extraordinary tale of the human who deeply loved an android. They marveled at the sight of Xavier, his unwavering devotion etched into every line of his frozen form, a guardian forever bound to those he held most dear. In this way, the story of Renn, Jenny, and Xavier became a beacon of hope, a reminder that love knows no boundaries and that true friendship can transcend even the vastness of the cosmos itself.

Chapter 16: PLANET EARTH

Curiosity gnawed at Jeremy. Twenty years. Two decades since he'd last seen his brother's face. From his vantage point atop a stack of crates, he peered down at the disembarking passengers. A motley crew they were – spacefarers of every stripe, their clothes a vibrant tapestry of cultures. Yet, his attention snagged on two figures who stood out from the rest. Identical uniforms, stark and severe, encased their forms, shrouding them in an air of mystery.

Catching sight of his brother, Tim raised his arm and waved. He pointed to Jeremy and said something to the soldier with him.

Time seemed to rewind as the two brothers collided in a fierce hug. Despite being the elder, Jeremy found himself enveloped in the warmth of Tim's embrace. The roles had reversed – Tim, once the skinny kid he had to protect, now towered over him, his strength evident as he lifted Jeremy off the ground.

"You grow taller every time I see you," Jeremy said with amazement and brotherly pride as Tim stood him back on his feet, the room still spinning from the exuberant embrace. Despite the years that had passed, Jeremy couldn't help but see flashes of the little boy he had once known in Tim's features. Yet, there was an undeniable transformation – the once scrawny kid had grown into a towering figure, his broad shoulders and confident stance vastly different from the timid youth Jeremy remembered.

"Naw," Tim laughed. "You're shrinking with old age." Tim moved his gaze towards the soldier beside him. "I'd like you to meet Lieutenant Comstock."

Applying a small amount of pressure, Jeremy grasped the hand of the other being in uniform. "It's a pleasure to meet you, Lieutenant." He glanced over the being's body shape and features. "Human, Lieutenant?"

"Yes. And call me Opal."

"I don't remember you on the space station," Jeremy said. "And you appear too old to have been born here on New Earth. May I ask about your origins?"

Tim chuckled. Opal smiled. "You and your brother think alike. That was the first question Tim asked me. I was born on the station during the third year of our journey. I would have been too young for either of you to pay attention to either on the station or here on New Earth. But you might remember my parents or oldest sister. My parents were George and Darlene Comstock. My dad was a member of the aviation team. Nicole Comstock was my oldest sister. She would have been several grades below you."

"Wing Wizard Comstock?" Jeremy's jaw dropped. "Your dad was THE Wing Wizard Comstock? I grew up on his wing designs! I worked alongside him for years. The man was a genius and came up with ideas that even Xavier scratched his head over. Irreplaceable, that's what he was. It's a pleasure to meet you." Jeremy vigorously shook her hand up and down.

"Perhaps you can show her your pleasure by not breaking her hand," Tim teased, his eyes twinkling.

"Oh, sorry." Jeremy let go of her hand. "So, Little Brother, what brings you to New Earth?"

"Xavier sent for me."

"Xavier?" Jeremy asked. "What does he want?"

"He wouldn't say. He said he needed someone for an important mission and that I was perfect for the job."

"Are you also the perfect person?" Jeremy asked, addressing Opal.

"I do not know," Opal said. "Head Commander Xavier gave no reason for his choice of me, only that a second human was required. I happened to be available."

"What does he want with two humans?" Jeremy asked.

"We'll find out soon. We're to rendezvous at twenty-one hundred on the station."

"Reporting as requested," Tim said as he entered Xavier's office, bringing his right hand to his forehead.

"Welcome aboard," Xavier said, extending his hand. "Remember, this is not a military ship. No saluting is necessary."

"In that case, I'd say a hug is necessary." Tim walked over and placed both arms around the android. Even though Tim had grown over the years, Xavier still towered over him.

Xavier wrapped his arms around the human, although the act of hugging still did not bring him joy. "I am glad to see you, Tim. You look more like your grandfather every day."

"That's what Mother says," Tim said, releasing his embrace and taking a seat.

Xavier extended his hand to the female human. "You must be Tim's partner.'

"Yes, Sir. My name is Lieutenant. . . I mean, Opal Comstock. It's a pleasure to meet you, Head Commander. Tim has told me so much about you."

Xavier lowered his eyelids as he stared at the male human. "A word of advice. Don't believe everything Tim tells you. He exaggerates."

"I do not!" Tim said.

"Might I remind you about the flying squirrel incident?"

"Well, maybe that one time." Tim and Xavier laughed. Opal's head snapped back, her eyebrows flying upwards in a question mark.

"You seem surprised, Opal. Have you never heard an android laugh?" Xavier asked.

"Yes, a few times," Opal said. "But they just chuckle. You did a full-blown belly laugh. Tim said you are different from other AIs."

"That I am. I am the only one of my kind. There was another, but she passed some years ago."

"Tim's grandmother, Jenny."

"Correct. Tim has informed you of his past."

"I wasn't sure what you needed us for, so I thought it best to apprise her of mine and your past," Tim said.

"A reasonable conclusion."

"So why did you send for us?"

"What I am about to tell you cannot leave this room. Three days ago, at 0-fifteen hundred, the ISC received a signal from Earth," Xavier said. "It lasted for three minutes, then ended. Two hours later, it was received again for the duration of time – three minutes. The signal continued at this exact interval for forty-eight hours, then ceased. No further transmissions have been received since 0-fifteen hundred yesterday."

"After all this time?" Tim asked. "What's it been? Forty years?"

"Thirty-eight. ISC Headquarters was quite surprised to receive the signal."

"What did the message say?" Opal asked.

"That's the strangest part," Xavier replied. "The ISC received only a signal; no message was attached. They believe one of two possibilities has occurred: one, things on Earth have gone terribly wrong, and they cannot send an actual message. The second possibility, although unlikely, is that the transmitters we left behind have malfunctioned."

"If memory is correct, the ISC left something like thirty transmitters behind," Tim said.

"Thirty-six, to be exact," Xavier stated.

"I can't believe they would all malfunction," Opal said. The androids designed them to last for a million years."

"That was the ISC's thought as well." Xavier placed a large envelope on the table. "They want a small company of three humans and three security androids to make the trip to Earth and investigate. If problems exist, they believe humans will respond better to their own kind. Our last encounters with the humans did not go well if you remember."

"Oh, I remember," Tim said, recalling the days he and his family were held against their will. And the reaction to his grandfather and Glogg at the UN Assembly. "Who is the third human?"

"A member of ISC Security," Xavier answered. "You will pick him up on Zaylara Prime. His name is Robert Hellsworth. He was born on the station forty-six years before we left, lived on Earth by choice for thirty years, and served in the French military. When we arrived at New Earth, he continued his security career with ISC. He is skilled in negotiations and will be the one to talk with the humans and analyze the situation."

"And our duty?" Tim asked.

"Even though this is not a military assignment, you will be under the authority of the ISC. As such, certain criteria and protocols must be maintained. You, Timothy, will oversee the mission.

Everyone, including the androids, will report to you. However, as you are aware, the androids have authority over your safety and will provide any military support." Xavier looked at the two humans before him. They seemed so young, yet he had full confidence in them. "We have no way of knowing what awaits you on Earth or what you will discover. Trust Robert, but rely on your own gut feelings. They have always served you well. Never go anywhere without the security droids. If one of them tells you something is too dangerous, do not argue but do as they say."

"Who's the android in charge?" Tim asked.

"I am," came a familiar voice. Tim turned to see Juaquin walk through the door.

"I was hoping you'd be joining us," Tim said, giving the large android a hug. "It's been too long, Juaquin. How are you doing?"

"I am operating in accordance with my parameters," Juaquin answered.

"Same out Juaquin," Tim laughed. "How many androids are going with us?"

"Six more besides myself," Juaquin said. "All top-of-the-line security droids whose main purpose is to project you two and Mr. Hellsworth."

"So, when do we leave?"

"In two hours," Xavier said.

"That soon?" Tim commented. "Doesn't leave any time for a family visit."

"Sorry, not this time. But I promise you a nice, long visit when you return." Xavier handed Tim a sealed envelope.

"What's this? "

"Specs on your mission," Xavier answered. "ISC's expectations. Scenarios and how to manage them. Anything and everything we could think of is inside there." The two humans gave questionable looks.

"Then I guess we should head to our ship," Tim said

The Head Commander stood and outstretched his hand. "I wish you the best of luck on your mission."

This time, Tim shook the android's hand. "I look forward to seeing you again upon our return." Tim turned, paused, and turned back around. "By the way, is it going to take us five years to make the journey like when we came here and another five to return?"

Xavier laughed again. "Not this time. Thanks to technical advancements, the trip will only take a year and a half each way. Add another three to six months to complete your assessment of Earth's situation, and I estimate we will meet again in about three and a half years. Since I do not age and you will age little due to space travel, I suspect we will not be much older. And, Tim, one more thing. After what happened last time, do not expect the humans to greet you or the androids with open arms."

"I'm way ahead of you on that one, Sir. I remember their reactions that day when Glogg and my grandfather addressed them at the UN Assembly. Plus, I am sure they have not forgiven us for leaving them behind."

————————

Tim and Opal walked down the hallway toward hanger number 8, their duffle bag of clothing and toiletries slung over their shoulders. As they turned the corner, Tim's eyes grew to the size of half-dollars.

"Is that what I think it is?" Tim asked, staring at the gay airship docked at the walkway.

"It's the latest model of the V-647 inter-stellular airship you helped design," Juaquin said "The engineers did a few modifications to help with our mission that I think you'll like."

"She looks awfully small," Opal said. "Are you sure it can accommodate all ten of us, our food, supplies, and communication equipment?"

"Since androids do not need to eat, our supplies are minimal," Juaquin said. "And we do not need to rest and have daily activities. We could easily accommodate thirty androids inside if there were no humans aboard." Juaquin saw the skeptical look that remained on Opal's face. "I assure you, Miss, the ship is of sufficient size and comfort."

"Opal," the female said. "Call me Opal."

"Shall we go aboard, Opal?"

Opal stepped up to the door and heard the familiar "swoosh" as it opened. "Xavier said she can get us to Earth in a year and a half, is that correct?"

"I would estimate more like fourteen months," Juaquin said. "I'll show you to your quarters and then take you to the bridge to meet your crew."

"Sir, Earth should be within viewing range in another thirty minutes," Samuel stated.

"Which one is she?" Opal asked, her body filled with hundreds of needles pricking her skin.

"That large body to the left," Samuel said. "Hue, raise the magnification to 100 plus."

Robert, the third human, moved closer to the observation window. "I can't wait to see her. I always hoped I would return one day. She's such a beautiful planet."

All three stared out the window as the image grew in size and clarity, their insides filled with butterflies, feeling like kids in a candy shop. Opal gave a light giggle at the joy of seeing, at last, the blue planet her parents called home.

An image of a dull, brown planet filled the screen. Two-thirds of the surface was filled with liquid, but it was a dirty gray, not the blue they expected. It appeared incapable of sustaining life. Above the equator, no green existed. The land was black and charred. Even the northern ice cap was a dingy gray.

"Samuel, I think your instruments are malfunctioning," Jeremy said. "That can't be Earth. Where's the blue seas and white clouds?"

Samuel checked his readings. "My instruments confirm that this is indeed Earth, Sir."

"That doesn't look like the Earth we learned about in school," Opal said.

"Or the Earth I lived on," Robert said. Samuel, can you increase the magnification? Maybe we're getting some space interference, altering Earth's colors."

"Raising magnification another two hundred," Hue stated.

Another image appeared on the viewing screen, and this one was more horrifying than the first. Huge blast holes the size of a football field filled the landscapes. The Great Lakes, Lake Victoria, and other northern hemisphere reservoirs were waterless and sunbaked. Cracked mud fields filled their basins. The great forests were replaced with dead zones. The Himalayas, Rocky Mountains, and the Alps rose mere yards toward the sky, and their great stone foundations blasted away. Great cities like New York, Paris, Chicago, England, Madrid, and the Kremlin lay in rubble, their bare steel ribs shining in the dimmed sun. Not a single building remained intact on any northern continent. A worldwide cloud of dust and ash encircled Earth, blocking out a substantial portion of the sun.

"What in the hell happened here?" Tim asked. "Did the Kett come back and start harvesting the planet?

"Sir, I'm picking up a high degree of radiation in the northern hemisphere," Hue reported.

"Continue our course, but stay twelve killigs above the planet," Robert ordered. "Tell me if the radiation levels rise. Keep the deflectors to a maximum. Run a scan and check for any signs of life, either animal or plant."

"Yes, Sir."

Tim remained silent as they neared the brown planet. His heart pumped faster with every minute that ticked by. He prayed that the scene he was witnessing was a mistake. Unable to maintain his composure, he began to pace around the room as his grandfather often did in times of stress.

After fifteen minutes, Hue gave his report. "Sir, I detect no life forms, either plant or animal, above the equator."

"None?"

"No, Sir. Not even a blade of grass."

"What about below the equator?"

"I am unable to scan the southern hemisphere from this trajectory. I'll need to change our heading to scan the southern Earth."

"Make it so."

After a long ten minutes, Hue reported, "I am detecting signs of both animal and plant life below the equator, although on a reduced scale from what our records show."

"Are any of them human?" Tim asked.

"Yes, although sporadic. Around the 20th parallel south, I detect a limited number of humans. Below the Tropic of Capricorn across Africa and South America is a larger accumulation, with the largest concentrated at the south pole. I estimate the combined total to be one million two hundred and fifteen."

"Just over a million?" Robert asked.

Hearing the news, Tim collapsed in a nearby chair. "The Northern leaders finally did it – blew themselves up. Out of over eight billion lives, only a little over a million remain. How did they let this happen?"

Watch for Guardians of Earth III

in December, 2024.

.

Please leave an honest review on Amazon. It helps me write better when I understand what you liked and didn't like.

ABOUT THE AUTHOR

P.R. Garcia grew up in rural Michigan and is the youngest of three. She became a lover of Science Fiction at an early age when her parents took her to the movies. When she heard Patricia Neal tell the robot Gort in The Day the Earth Stood Still "Klaatu barada nikto," she was hooked. Inspired by what was possible, she and her dog spent many days fighting aliens and investigating new planets in the fields behind her home. Her love continued to grow, and in high school, the series Star Trek hit television, boosting her fascination with what might exist in space. Her friends still comment on how she skipped the football games to stay home to watch each episode. She became an award-winning basket weaver in her thirties and continued in this craft for three decades. After retiring from her thirty-year job, she moved to San Diego, California. She volunteered for five years as a guide on the Whale Watching Boats, teaching people from around the world about the Pacific Ocean's aquatic life.

At sixty-two, Ms. Garcia wrote her Europa Saga, a compelling, ten-part sci-fi series of intrigue, suspense, and mystery. The Saga is a new and fresh retelling of the story of Atlantis and its inhabitants. Her story launched her into the world of a best-selling author.

Global warming, deforestation, pollution of our air and water, species loss, and the devastation of Earth itself are all subjects dear to Ms. Garcia's heart. She has incorporated those themes into her later books, including books seven through nine of the Europa Saga and Extinction 2038.

Ms. Garcia also writes children's books and is the author of the Granny Duck series. In addition, she designs adult coloring books.

For more information or to sign up for her newsletter, go to her web page: http://www.prgarcia1.com.

If you would like more information about her books, please click here:

https://prgarcia1.ck.page/17008c49c4

OTHER BOOKS BY P.R. GARCIA

The Europa Saga - She was never meant to be human.

When a young woman regains consciousness, she is told her mother was assassinated, and she is the next target.

The Europa Saga is a fresh telling of the myth of Atlantis, who its people were, and why they sank the city. Told through the eyes of a twenty-year-old human female named Europa, the saga covers four generations and spans over two thousand years.

As Europa tries to grip her mother's death, she discovers the truth - her entire life has been a fabrication, an intricate weave of lies and omissions. Her parents are thousands of years old and have been on Earth, along with her caregivers, for over two thousand years. They are not human but the royal leaders of an aquatic race of aliens from Jupiter's ice moon, Europa. Forced to flee their homeworld due to civil war, they remain hidden in the depths of the Pacific Ocean in the technically advanced City of Atlantis. But their numbers are dwindling. Because of a chemical attack by their mortal enemy, who tracks them to Earth, no Atlantean child has survived past the age of five. When Queen Medaron miraculously becomes pregnant, the child's only hope is to be born as a human.

Europa must discover who and what she is and learn the authentic story of her people. As the new queen, she protects them from the enemy that still hunts them and hidden from the world of humans. But to do that, she must become an Atlantean herself and lose her humanity. If she fails, she will die, and the Atlanteans will be no more. For information about the Europa Saga, go to http://europasaga.com

Extinction 2038: Over half of the ice in Antarctica has melted, revealing the corpse of a dinosaur. A group of paleontologists stumble across it, believing they have found the find of the century. But inside the corpse is the original strain of Ebola. As the disease spreads across the globe, killing most animals and man, society breaks down. Three scientists with a cure are stranded in Antarctica with no one alive to rescue them and no internet to call for help.

The Bounty Hunter: Sold into slavery as a child, rescued, and adopted by the Kolorian Huntsmen, BiiJun is trained in the ancient Creed of Taung defenses and discipline. A Bounty Hunter, known only as "The Hunter," he is the top Pursuer in the quadrant. Hidden behind his helmet and armor, he always gets his bounty—until now. An encounter from his past is destroying his soul and haunting his every waking and sleeping minute.

Knowing he cannot go forward without rectifying his past, The Dominee sends him on a mission to Rigel Three. There, he is forced to confront his former actions and make one of two choices: continue as a Bounty Hunter or remove his armor and adopt a new lifestyle. Only one choice will bring hope and peace to the galaxy. Will he make the right decision?

For more information, go to http://www.prgarcia1.com

Or check her books on Amazon at Amazon.com: P.R. Garcia

Please leave an honest review on Amazon.